# Rosa of Linden Castle.

## A TALE FOR PARENTS AND CHILDREN

by Christoph von Schmid
author of
*The Basket of Flowers.*

Lamplighter Publishing
Waverly, Pennsylvania.

Rosa of Linden Castle.

Published by Lamplighter Publishing; a division of Cornerstone Family Ministries, Inc.

The Lamplighter Rare Collector's Series is a collection of family Christian literature from the 17th, 18th, and 19th centuries. Each edition is printed in an attractive hard-bound collector's format.

For more information, call us at 1-888-246-7735, visit us at www.lamplighterpublishing.com or write:

Lamplighter Publishing
P.O. Box 777
Waverly, PA 18471

Author: Christoph von Schmid
Translated and edited: A.H. Lochman, 1845
Printed by Jostens in the United States of America
Arrestox 53500 Green, API 4014s Peruvian Gold, Crown Roll Leaf 11146

ISBN 1-58474-025-6

# Rosa of Linden Castle.

# Rosa of Linden Castle.

## Chapter One.

### ROSA'S EARLY HISTORY.

N the southern borders of Swabia, a country famed for its blooming vales, its mighty mountain ranges, and its lofty glaciers, which even in mid-summer raised their shining peaks to the clouds, in days of old stood the splendid castle of Linden, on the towering cliffs of a rugged mountain. Centuries after, its dilapidated towers of moss-covered walls attracted the attention of the passing traveller, and recalled to mind its history.

This castle was once the home of Edelbert, as noble and brave a knight as ever wielded a sword and lance, yet underneath whose iron armor beat a warm and benevolent heart. The Duke of Swabia honored him with special marks of friendship, and even the emperor himself regarded him with peculiar approbation. His wife Matilda, by her intelligence, her piety, her virtues, and her kindness to the poor, gained the esteem and regard of all around. In consequence of the unsettled and warlike state of affairs, Edelbert spent but little time at the castle with his family, but accompanied the duke in his campaigns against the hordes of marauders which disturbed the peace and quiet of his domains.

During the absence of her husband, Matilda found her greatest pleasure in the company of their only child, a promising daughter, whose name was Rosa. To train up this child, and give her mind and heart a right direction, was her chief care. Her mode of instruction was simple and natural, and on that account the most impressive and pleasing. Being herself pious, and deeply interested in those things which she sought to impress upon the mind of her child, it was to her not an irksome but a pleasant duty.

Her first object was to make her child acquainted with the character and goodness of God, and to awaken and call forth in her tender heart a sincere regard and filial affection towards her heavenly Father. An ardent admirer of the works of nature, her own mind was often led through nature up to nature's God. From the windows of her parlor in the castle, there was a most delightful prospect; here she frequently sat with her needlework, and with delight and feelings of reverence towards the Creator of all, gazed upon the majestic glaciers as they sparkled in the sunbeams, upon the vine-clad hills, the blooming vales, and the meandering streams. From these she took occasion to direct the attention of her daughter to the wisdom, the power, and the goodness of God.

On one occasion, a beautiful summer's morning, she awoke Rosa very early, saying, "Rosa, my dear, come and see how beautifully and majestically the sun rises; behold those golden-tinged clouds, and those silvered mountains of our church in the village, as it rises amidst the tall linden trees with which it is surrounded. The happy husbandmen, refreshed by sleep, are hurrying to the labors of the day. There the whistling shepherd's boy is driving his flocks to the grassy hills – there the mowers are cutting the sweet-smelling grass – there the yellow grain-fields are waving ready for the sickle – everywhere we see the wisdom and goodness of our God. How great, how incomprehensible, and how good, must He not be, who looks upon all his creatures with benevolence and compassion; who provides alike for the poor peasant who lives in his straw-thatched cottage, and for us who dwell in a castle; who created this earth and fitted it for the abode of man; who giveth seed to the sower and bread to the eater, and who has also made provision for our salvation, that when we leave this world we may live with him in heaven for ever." Rosa was deeply impressed with what her mother said, and involuntarily folding her hands, exclaimed, "Oh! how good and great art Thou who hast made all things for our good."

In a similar manner, Matilda taught her daughter to look from the creature to the Creator. From all his works – from the dewdrop as it glittered upon the leaf, to the sun in the heavens, in whose rays it basked – from the changing seasons, with the beauties and blessings which they brought – from all, she took occasion to teach Rosa useful lessons, and impress her mind with the goodness of God to us, and our duty and obligations to him, so that she could scarcely look upon a flower, or eat an apple or a peach, without being reminded of the instructions of her mother.

Whilst engaged in some useful employment this pious mother repeated to her daughter such interesting histories from the Bible, as were suited to her age and comprehension. Rosa listened with the deepest interest to the temptation and fall of our first parents in Paradise; to the histories of the patriarchs to the dealings of God with his ancient people, the Israelites; how he led them through the wilderness and established them in a land which flowed with milk and honey, and how he ever manifested his displeasure at all that was evil, and his approbation of all that was good. The lives of bad men which the Scriptures set forth, she was taught to regard as warnings, and the lives of good men as examples worthy of her imitation. Especially was she delighted to hear her mother speak of the Saviour. With the angels and the shepherds, she rejoiced to see the babe of Bethlehem in the manger, and with the wise men of the east, she offered to him, in child-like simplicity, the grateful emotions of a heart touched with his love, — an offering far more precious in his sight than gold, frankincense, and myrrh. She noticed his affectionate regard and prompt obedience to his parents, and how he grew in favor with God and man; and formed the most determined resolution never to displease and disobey her parents, and to grow better every day. In spirit she accompanied the divine Teacher in his journeyings through the Holy Land; stood among his hearers on the mountain, or at the sea, or in the temple; treasured up his instructions in her mind, and promised her mother to obey his teachings. She was particularly pleased to hear that Jesus felt a deep interest in children; that on one occasion he called little children to him and blessed them, and on another restored a little girl, who had died, to her weeping parents; and that he called to life a young man, whom they were carrying to his grave, and gave him to his sorrowing and widowed mother and she felt inclined to seek his blessing, to love and trust in Him, who is able to wipe every tear from the eye, to help in every time of need, to deprive even death of his terrors, and give eternal life to those that believe on him. When her mother spoke of the sufferings which the innocent Jesus took upon himself, out of love to the perishing and guilty, and how, when bleeding and dying, he prayed his heavenly Father to forgive his murderers, she was melted to tears, and determined to consecrate herself entirely to Him who loved her and gave himself for her. Thus this pious mother taught her daughter to know and love her God, and her divine Redeemer.

Matilda, however, desired also, next to the knowledge and love of God, to teach her daughter to love all men; and especially to love and obey her parents. Her deep affection for her daughter could not fail to call forth as deep an affection in return. Though her father was not much at home, yet as her mother always spoke of him in the most affectionate terms, Rosa ardently and sincerely loved him. It was a sufficient motive to obedience, for her mother to say, "Rosa, my child, conduct yourself in such a manner that when your dear father comes home, I may be able to give him a good account of you." And when her father occasionally came home, Rosa and her mother exerted themselves to the utmost to render him happy.

An instance of her desire to please her father, we will relate. Near the wall, which enclosed the castle, stood a favorite peach tree, bearing the most delicious fruit. One season it bare but few peaches, but these were peculiarly fine. During her father's absence her mother pulled the fruit and divided it into three parcels; one for the father, another for herself, and another for Rosa; adding, however, at the same time, "My share I will save for your father." Rosa replied. "He shall have mine also," and upon no consideration could she be prevailed upon to eat one of them; but procured from her mother a neat little basket, arranged them, interspersed with flowers, most tastefully in it, and presented them to him as soon as he returned.

Matilda felt a deep interest in the poor and destitute of her neighbourhood, and frequently visited them, to converse with and aid them, at times with a little money, but more frequently with the necessaries of life. On these excursions she generally took Rosa with her, in order to awaken feelings of benevolence and sympathy in her bosom, and on many occasions distributed her charities through the hands of her daughter, that by experience she might learn the blessedness of giving to the poor. She desired to teach her child that it is our duty to sacrifice many of our pleasures and enjoyments for the good of others. On the occasion of her birthday, her father presented her with a piece of money, telling her she might purchase with it whatever she pleased.

Rosa was delighted, and thought of many things she would like to buy, and she asked her mother what she should do; her mother mentioned a great many pretty things she could get for her money, but Rosa scarcely knew what to choose. Whilst they were thus engaged, a poor widow entered the room, and told her tale of woe. She had several small children to support, and she depended mainly upon the sale of a little butter, and the milk of her cow; but her cow died, and she did not know what would become of her and her little ones.

The pious lady replied, "My dear woman, I feel
for you, but I have lately assisted so many in similar
circumstances, that I shall not be able to replace your
entire loss; you shall, however, have what I am able
to spare."

She went and brought some money and counted
it on the table, adding, "If you had but a few dollars
more, you could buy another cow."

No sooner did Rosa hear this, than she ran and
brought the piece of money that her father had given
her on her birthday, and presented it to the woman,
saying to her mother, "I can do better without those
trinkets and fineries which I intended to buy with this
money, than this poor woman and her children can do
without a cow."

The woman wept for joy, and kissed Rosa's hand
in token of her gratitude. When the woman had left,
Matilda embraced her daughter, and said, "My child,
your active sympathy and self-denial for others' good,
is worth more than a thousand such pieces of gold, and
more than all the trinkets and fineries in the world."

This good woman sought to cultivate a habit of
cheerful and ready obedience in her daughter, from
her earliest childhood; "for," she said, "self-will is the
greatest barrier to all that is good. A child must first
learn to submit its own will to the will of its parents;
then it will be better prepared and more ready to
submit its own will to the will of God; for if it yield
not obedience to, and acquiesce not in the will of its
parents, whom it constantly sees, how shall it yield
obedience to acquiesce in the will of God, whom it
does not see? The ardent desires of the child must be

at times restrained, and self-will must be subdued; so that the seeds and germs of nobler and holier feelings and desires may spring up, and come to maturity." She was prompt and firm in refusing to yield her assent to any thing which she thought improper and wrong; and though Rosa often sought to gain, with tears and repeated entreaties, what her mother at first refused, yet she soon found it was all in vain, and that her mother would never break her word. A prompt obedience was always insisted on; whenever her mother bid her do any thing, all other engagements and amusements had immediately to be laid aside and the command of her mother obeyed. No flowers in the garden, or fruit from the trees, was she permitted to pluck without her permission. Matilda, however, did not unnecessarily cross the wishes of her child, nor impose upon her any needless commands, for fear she might perplex her mind, and lose the powerful hold she had upon her affection. "Few commands are required," said she, "but these must be rigidly enforced. God gave but ten commandments to the children of men, and if these were universally obeyed, few others would be necessary."

Matilda soon found that to ensure obedience, promises of rewards and threatenings of punishment were required. It is thus that our heavenly father incites us, his older children, to obedience, and deters us from evil. It afforded her the greatest pleasure to give Rosa some of the choicest fruit of the garden, but she had always to conduct herself so as to deserve it. For example, at one time she said, "My child, if you learn your lesson well, this morning, I will give you a plate of our excellent May-dukes." At another time, "If you hem this handkerchief neatly, you shall have a bunch of grapes." The task was generally well done, and the satisfaction of having merited the approbation of her dear mother, greatly enhanced the value of the gift she received. When Rosa committed a fault, or did any thing wrong, it was a sufficient punishment for her to be refused to accompany her mother in some little excursion of pleasure. And when her mother appeared grieved, and said "I did not expect such conduct from my child," Rosa could not rest, until her mother had forgiven her, and appeared pleased again.

Idleness was regarded by this excellent woman as the source of much evil and many vices, hence she was always engaged in some useful employment herself, and gave her child such employment as was suited to her years and her taste. She was accustomed to say, "What my child can do, is indeed not of much importance in itself, but she is thus forming habits of industry, and her mind and time are employed on something useful and innocent, which might otherwise be occupied with that which is hurtful and evil." Matilda, as was customary in those days, superintended the management of all her domestic concerns herself, and was anxious that her daughter might be qualified to do the same; hence she instructed her in all the necessary duties of a good house-keeper. She was particularly fond of attending to the garden, of cultivating flowers and vegetables; especially as moderate exercise in the open air was conducive to her health. Her mother gave her a small spot of ground as her own, and procured her a little rake, and a neat little watering-pot. With these she was much pleased, and spent some time every day in sowing seeds and setting out plants, and weeding her own little garden. When her mother had a mess of peas boiled, which Rosa had raised, she said, "Mother, these are the sweetest peas I ever ate."

"They taste the sweeter," said her mother, "because you raised them; it is thus God rewards industry and diligence. The bread of diligence is always sweeter than the bread of idleness. The poor, laborious husbandman eats his coarse bread with a greater relish, than the idle rich man the choicest dainties."

This excellent mother judiciously varied the employments of Rosa, so that they never became dull and irksome to her. Nor did she approve the course taken by many parents of refusing her any recreations and innocent enjoyments. "Children," she said, "must have some time for play and amusement, but their amusements must be judiciously selected for them." Hence, she occasionally invited some little girls of Rosa's age to spend an afternoon with her. Among these, was one of a mild and amiable disposition, whose name was Agnes. The plays and amusements chosen for them were such as required healthful exercise of body, and also the exercise of judgment and reflection, so that even the hours of recreation were of great advantage to the children. "Try and make your children contented and happy, and they will the more readily and cheerfully obey your commands, and the more highly esteem and dearly love you." Such was the advice this devoted mother gave to parents, and this the principle upon which she based her instructions.

Most assiduously did Matilda guard the heart of her daughter against the first appearance of vanity and pride of dress. On one occasion, when the duke and his lady, and a number of noble families visited them, it was thought proper that Rosa should appear in a manner becoming her station in life. She was clothed in a most costly silk, and wore a splendid necklace studded with diamonds. During the course of the evening, Rosa was much admired on account of her personal charms, and the richness of her dress. Fearful lest the compliments paid to her might have an evil tendency, she, after the company had gone, said to her, "I was much grieved to hear the compliments the ladies and gentlemen paid to you. Could they perceive nothing for which to praise you, but your beauty and the finery you had on, which are now again laid aside! Their praises were due to the manufacturer and jeweler, but not to you. And beauty and charms of person are gifts of God, bestowed, sometimes, upon the most vicious and vulgar, and, at best, must soon fade and pass away. Oh, my child, if I could perceive nothing else in you, to deserve commendation, I would be the most miserable of parents. Dear Rosa, seek to possess such a disposition and such virtues as must ever command esteem. What are these fine things, compared to a well cultivated mind, a virtuous heart, and a life of benevolence! These are the jewels with which we are to be adorned; let your adorning not be that outward adorning of plaiting the hair, and of wearing of gold, or of putting on of apparel, but the ornament of a meek and quiet spirit, which is, in the sight of God, of great price."

What rendered these instructions peculiarly efficacious, was, that they were enforced by example. The life of this excellent mother was like a pure unclouded mirror, in which the daughter could see reflected the spirit and virtues which should adorn her character. Her whole conduct was a pleasing commendation of all her instructors. She was discreet, modest, and unassuming. She never spake in commendation of herself; never prided herself upon her station, her wealth, her virtues; never gave way to passion, never spake ill of any, nor repeated the ill reports she heard of others. She frequently took her daughter with her to the throne of grace, and so warm were her expressions of gratitude for mercies received, and so fervent her petitions to God for blessings upon her husband, her child, herself, and upon all mankind, that the impressions made upon Rosa's mind were never effaced. She saw the beauty and excellency of religion exhibited before her eyes in the daily conduct of her mother, and was firmly resolved, by God's grace, to imitate the example and imbibe the spirit of her dear parent.

Such instruction, and such an example, could not fail, under the blessing of God, to produce the happiest results. Rosa grew up, a pattern of every excellence, a beautiful copy for the model set before her, the joy of her parents, and a blessing to all around.

## Chapter Two.

### THE DEATH OF ROSA'S MOTHER.

ROSA was not permitted to enjoy the happiness of possessing so excellent a mother for a very long time. She was about fourteen years old when her mother suddenly became dangerously ill. She felt her danger, and did not conceal it from her daughter. "Rosa," said she, "send a messenger in haste for your father; I desire to see him once more before I die. Send also for our pious pastor, Norbert. He will not refuse to bring consolation to me in my dying hour. It might indeed have been too late, if I had delayed my preparation for eternity to this hour. Our whole life is to be devoted to this important work. This is its principal design; for this purpose God has placed us in this world.

The pious pastor, a venerable old man, immediately obeyed the summons, and was soon at the bedside of this member of his fold; and after some conversation, in which he endeavored to strengthen her faith, and encourage her hope and confidence in her Redeemer, he offered up a most fervent prayer in her behalf. He spake with such a firm conviction, such a lively impression of the power of divine grace and of the blessed realities of eternity, that Rosa almost desired to die and go with her dear mother.

Rosa never left her mother, but, like a ministering angel, anticipated her every want, and cheerfully and affectionately did every thing in her power, to render her as comfortable as possible. On the second day of Matilda's illness, Edelbert reached the castle at a late hour in the night. When he was announced, Rosa ran to meet him at the outer gate; her heart was so full that she could only exclaim, "Oh, father! Father! My mother! My mother!"

Edelbert with a trembling heart hastened to his wife's chamber. He was alarmed to see her pale and deathly countenance, and gave vent to the feelings of his heart in a flood of tears. Rosa stood weeping on the other side of the bed. Not a word was spoken for a few minutes. At length the dying woman, with a heavenly smile on her countenance, reached one hand to her husband, and with the other grasped the hand of her daughter. "Dearest Edelbert, dearest Rosa," said she, with a tremulous voice, "my hour has come. I shall not live to see another rising sun. Weep not for me! Death will be my gain. In our Father's house on high, there are many mansions. I shall only go to another, a blessed home. We shall not long be separated. We shall soon meet again, and never, never part." Her voice now began to fail, and, overcome with the exertions that she had made, she sank back upon her pillow.

After a little, she recovered from her swoon, and said, "Dearest husband, behold our child. Never have I given you a likeness of myself as a memento of affection. Let this our daughter be to you a living likeness; the best pledge of my affection, and the most impressive and pleasing memento I can possibly give you. To you, in my dying moments, in the presence of God, I commit and intrust her. It has been my constant aim to train her up in the fear of the Lord. Do complete in her what I have commenced. Rectify the errors I may have committed in her education. I most heartily thank you for the many proofs you have given me of your kindness and affection; and pray you, for my sake, to transfer the affection you have ever borne towards me to our beloved daughter.

"And you, dearest Rosa," continued she, "you have afforded me much happiness. You have been an affectionate and dutiful child. This testimony I must bear you in my dying hour. Oh! Cherish those principles of piety, those convictions of duty, which now possess your mind. Remain virtuous and good. Love God. Cleave to your blessed Redeemer. Obey his kind instructions. Avoid the very appearance of evil. Honor, love, esteem, and obey your dear Father. He is exposed to many dangers; and should he ever return from the field of battle wounded, supply my place, and take care of him. And in the decline of life be his stay, and support, and consolation. Remain an affectionate and dutiful child to him. Farewell."

"O God!" said she, casting an imploring look towards heaven," preserve Thou her from evil, and keep her in the ways of righteousness and truth! Hear this my last prayer—the fervent prayer of a mother's heart, now breaking in death, and let me meet her in heaven."

Edelbert and Rosa could contain themselves no longer; they wept aloud. The dying Christian joined the hands of father and daughter, and clasping them in her own, now icy cold, exclaimed, "We three have been of one heart and one mind in this world,—by the grace of God we shall be the same in the world to come. Death cannot extinguish our love. In heaven we shall live for ever, and for ever love each other."

Her countenance seemed to brighten with the hopes of heaven, and to be lighted up with the radiations of eternal glory; and casting one last, fond, lingering look upon her husband and daughter, she remarked, "My God is favoring me with great peace and joy in my dying hour; to Him be the praise. O my Rosa, how glad I am that you can see, in my death, how composed and happy they can die, who believe in our blessed Redeemer. Jesus Christ will not leave those who believe in him without comfort in that hour, when they need it most. I fear not death, I am already blessed in the sure hope of eternal life." Folding her hands, she again prayed in a scarcely audible voice, "As thou, blessed Redeemer, didst commend thy spirit into the hands of thy heavenly Father, so I now commit my spirit into thy hands." Her voice now failed her; the pale hue of death spread over her countenance; her eyes became fixed, and the spirit took its flight. Rosa stood at her side in speechless grief; and Edelbert amidst sobs and tears could only say, "She lived and died as a saint! She has now overcome the last enemy. May the Lord help us thus to live and thus to die, and bring us together in peace in his kingdom above." "Amen," responded Rosa.

We would not attempt to describe the distress and anguish of Edelbert and of the almost brokenhearted Rosa, during that night, on the following day, and at the funeral. The whole neighbourhood sympathized and wept with them. In the dwellings of the poor, who had lost in her their best earthly friend, there was much weeping and lamentation. The venerable and pious Norbert performed the funeral services. After he had addressed the immense concourse of people who had assembled, for a short time, the weeping and sobbing became so loud, that the voice of the preacher could no longer be heard; and being unable longer to restrain his own feelings, he raised his hands, and beckoned to the audience to be silent, and only added, "When tears and sobs speak so loud, I must be silent. Let us so live, that at our grave tears of affection and gratitude may loudly speak. Let us imbibe the spirit, and practice the virtues of the deceased, and like her be employed in works of faith and labors of love. Let us sow bountifully, then shall we also reap bountifully.

# Chapter Three.

## SEIZURE OF EDELBERT BY KUNERICK.

FTER the lapse of some time, the knight Edelbert was again called into active service. And one day, in the fall of the year, he returned to his castle severely wounded in the right arm. Rosa was much alarmed, and manifested the most tender regard and heartfelt sympathy for her beloved father. She was always near him. She prepared and brought him his food. She assisted in bandaging the wound; and as the arm healed but slowly, and time hung heavily upon him, because he was accustomed to an active mode of life, and felt that he ought to be at his post, in the service of his country, Rosa sought to engage his attention and to cheer his drooping spirits. Sometimes she would sit by his side with her needlework, and speak of her dear mother—recount to him the instructions she had imparted to her in his absence, the deeds of kindness and acts of charity she had performed, together with many incidents in her life, with which her father had not become acquainted. At other times she would ask him to relate to her events and circumstances which occurred in the wars; and thus she dispelled his gloom, rendered him cheerful, and the days of winter passed by, almost imperceptibly.

The flowers of spring had scarcely begun to put forth, when a noble knight appeared at the castle, to summon him to join the army. Edelbert anxiously desired to go, but felt that his arm was yet too weak to bear the sword or wield the lance. He nevertheless mustered all his men at the castle, and bade them hold themselves in readiness to march on the morning of the fourth day. Early in the morning of the appointed day he called them together in the large hall of the castle. Dressed in the splendid military costume of a knight, but without his armor, (for his wounded arm was yet too feeble to bear its weight) he appeared before his men, gave them over to the command of the knight who bore the summons, and exhorted them to act as men, and to render strict obedience to their officers. "Be brave as lions against your enemies, but gentle as lambs towards the poor and defenseless."

It was a matter of much grief to him that he could not accompany them. From the window of the castle he looked after them until they entered a wood, and were lost to his view. All that day he felt much dejected; the castle seemed lonely and deserted. After supper he sat musing in sadness before the fire. The evening was cold and damp. The storm-wind roared and the raindrops beat violently against the windows; and this added to the gloom of Edelbert's mind. Rosa, perceiving that her father was much cast down, tried every way in her power to rouse him and divert his attention. The fire on the hearth was stirred up and more fuel added. She then seated herself by his side and said: "Dear father, relate to me the history of the honest collier who visited you this afternoon. I know a little of his history—that he once lived with us, and that his daughter Agnes used to play with me, when we were children. I feel interested in the family, and am desirous of becoming more fully acquainted with their history."

"The history of my faithful Burkhard?" replied her father; "with the greatest pleasure! He was once a brave soldier and accompanied me in many a campaign, and stood by my side in many a hard-fought battle. The good man visited me this day. He knew that I would be dejected, because I could not accompany my men to the field of battle, and came to console and cheer me. "But before I relate his history, I must first tell you something of Kunerick, the knight of Forest castle. Of the splendid, well-fortified Forest castle you have often heard. From our windows in the upper hall, its lofty towers can be distinctly seen, as they rise above the tall pines with which it is surrounded. Kunerick you have never seen, for he has for a long time been my greatest enemy, and has never visited us. His enmity towards me took its rise from the following circumstance. He and I, as sons of noble families, were in early life summoned to the Duke's palace to attend upon his court. Kunerick, from a boy, was self-willed, passionate, and haughty, and on that account was not held in much esteem by any one. He envied me, because I was preferred before him. When we were able to bear arms, the duke, in order to try our skill in wielding the sword and the lance, invited the sons of noble families to a public contest. In this contest I obtained the first prize, a splendid sword with a gilt handle, which your dear mother was appointed to present to me, before all the nobles of Swabia. Kunerick, on that occasion, obtained a far inferior prize, a pair of silver spurs. From this time his heart was filled with hatred and envy towards me. But his hatred rose to its highest pitch when the Emperor, after a great battle, gave me, as a reward of my bravery, this gold medal, which I have ever since worn around my neck; and sharply reproved Kunerick for his rashness and inconsiderateness, by which we came near losing the day.

"The brave Burkhard was one of my bodyguards, and my constant companion in arms. He occupied a small cottage with a lot of land adjoining our possessions, and bordering on the forests of Kunerick. Kunerick was, however, a troublesome neighbour to Burkhard, as he kept a great quantity of game on his estates. The deer frequently came beyond his line of territory, and destroyed Burkhard's grain, and the wild hogs rooted up his meadow. The good man one day complained bitterly to me of the losses he thus sustained. I told him that he ought without hesitation to shoot whatever game he found off of Kunerick's grounds, because all that he found on my possessions, I had a right to claim.

"One evening, not long after this, as I was returning from the chase, with some of my servants, Burkhard's wife ran towards us with dishevelled hair, weeping aloud, wringing her hands, and begging me to help her if possible. Little Agnes was at her side, crying bitterly, 'Oh! My father, my father!' I was deeply affected, dismounted, took the poor woman by the hand, and inquired into the cause of her grief.

"The circumstances as she related them were briefly these. Burkhard, his wife, and Agnes were sitting at the door of their cottage, eating their supper of coarse bread and milk, little thinking of any danger; when, without any warning, Kunerick, accompanied by several armed servants, came upon them. The servants fell upon the poor man, tied his hands and feet, threw him upon a cart and drove off. This was done because Burkhard had lately shot a deer near the borders of Kunerick's forest, but on my possessions. This exasperated the knight so much that he swore he would catch the rascally poacher, as he called honest Burkhard, and cast him into the most dismal dungeon at his castle, there to perish with hunger and disease.

"'He shall be released,' I said, with no small degree of feeling, 'if to effect it I must storm Forest-castle.' I bade the weeping woman be of good cheer, and go with her child to my castle and stay there until I returned.

"I immediately started in pursuit of the murderous band, with the servants who were with me, hoping to overtake them before they should reach their destination. I sent on several men to reconnoiter, appointing a place where we would meet, whilst with the others I hastened, with full speed, towards Forest-castle. We were, however, soon met by the reconnoitering party, who stated that Kunerick was in a tavern not far from the road, drinking freely with his men, and that the cart on which Burkhard lay stood before the door. We consulted, for a moment, what we should do, and resolved to pass on, and secrete ourselves in a thick wood which skirted the road. We had not waited long before they came in sight. Not dreaming of any danger, they were in high spirits, singing and hallooing. In an instant we rushed upon them. The moon, having just risen, kindly undertook the office of lamp-bearer to give us light in our work of mercy and kindness. As they were not prepared for so sudden and impetuous an attack, and being somewhat under the influence of liquor, they made but feeble resistance, and soon took to flight. I could easily have taken Kunerick prisoner, but had compassion upon him, and suffered him to escape. Providently, no one was killed, though several were wounded, and the ground was strewed with the weapons of our enemies.

"We immediately unbound poor Burkhard, set him upon a horse that had thrown his rider in the skirmish, placed the arms and armor of our enemies which were left upon the ground on the cart, and, with mingled feelings of gratitude and joy, returned home. It is impossible to describe the delight of his wife and daughter, when they saw us entering the gate, with Burkhard riding at my side! And my joy was scarcely less than theirs; for I felt the satisfaction of having rescued a fellow-being from distress and misery.

"In order that they might not again be exposed to a similar danger, I took them, for a season, to the castle. Burkhard having been wounded in battle, was disqualified for the duty of bearing arms; yet, as he was able to do some light work, he could not bear the idea of eating the bread of idleness. In the deep recesses of the forest belonging to my estate, he found a little valley before unknown to any one, and not easily discovered; here he wished to live; and accordingly I built a small house for him there. He cleared a few acres of land, upon which he raised his bread, and with my permission follows the occupation of a collier. As the spot where he lives is so secluded, and as he is generally black with smoke and coal-dust, he feels himself perfectly secure from the attacks of Kunerick, and has never since been disturbed."

To this history, Edelbert added some examples of Burkhard's bravery and fidelity; and Rosa was so much interested in the facts related, that the fire had gone out, and the clock in the tower had struck twelve, before they thought of retiring to rest.

Just as they were preparing to go to bed, they heard an unusual noise. The arched gangways of the castle resounded with the voices of men and the rattling of their weapons. The heavy tread of men approaching the room in which Rosa and her father were sitting, were distinctly heard. Edelbert sprang up and reached his sword, and Rosa quickly bolted the door. But, in an instant, the door was broken open, and a well-armed knight, with three or four soldiers, stood before them.

"Now, Edelbert!" said the leader, with a thundering voice, his eyes flashing with rage, "the day of vengeance has come. I am Kunerick, whom you have so long insulted and abused. You shall now atone for your base conduct towards me. Bind him in chains and guard him well until we leave this place," said he to the soldiers. "The dungeon I had assigned to Burkhard shall be his abode. This castle now is mine: I shall select from its stores what appears to be of value to me, and then, my brave comrades, you may ransack the building, whilst I regale myself with the choicest of wines. Haste! In three hours we depart hence."

Rosa threw herself upon her knees before the cruel knight, and implored him to spare her father; but he only insulted her, and pushing her away, hastily left the room. Edelbert was bound and guarded by two soldiers.

Kunerick had watched his opportunity to glut his vengeance. He had heard that Edelbert had sent away the bravest of his men; and he succeeded in bribing some of those who yet remained, and gaining them over to his interest. By their means a secret passage, under ground, leading to the castle, was opened, and Kunerick entered without opposition.

## Chapter Four.

EDELBERT IS SEPARATED FROM HIS
DAUGHTER AND TAKEN TO
KUNERICK'S CASTLE.

DELBERT sat chained before the decaying embers on the hearth. Rosa knelt by his side, weeping, sobbing, and praying. She wrung her hands, and her dishevelled hair flowed in wild disorder over her face. She was almost distracted—all appeared to her like a wild dream of the night. The palace echoed with the boisterous merriment of the plundering and carousing soldiers, whilst the room in which Rosa and her father were confined was as silent and sombre as the sepulchre, being lighted up only by the glimmerings of the decaying lamp. The silence was broken only by the occasional and loud sigh which was wrung from the almost bursting bosom of Rosa.

"Oh!" exclaimed she, "How cruel to chain the hands so often employed in defending and rescuing the poor and needy—not even to spare his wounded arm. O Lord, help! O help us!"—was all she was able to say.

Edelbert, who, for a while, had not uttered a word, at last said to his daughter,—"Dearest child, try and compose yourself, and dry your tears. God, in his providence, has permitted his affliction to come upon us; let us kiss the hand with which he corrects us. He wounds in order that he may heal again. He will overrule this calamity for our good. We are in his

hands; against his will nothing can harm us. Even the
plottings of our enemies, He is able to turn to a good
account. Let us put our trust in Him. In times past, I
have rested my hopes of prosperity and happiness too
much on the favor of the Duke and the Emperor. I
have based my security upon the prowess of my own
arm; upon my sword and lance; upon the strength of
our castle; but henceforth I will look to God alone; He
shall be my defence and my fortress. We shall soon
part, my child," said he, putting his arm, laden with a
heavy chain, around her neck, and kissing her.

"Oh! Talk not of parting, dearest father," said Rosa.
"They shall not separate us! I will go with you to
prison and to death."

"No, my child," said her father, mildly; "Kunerick
will never allow you to accompany me; this request
he will never grant. Again I say we must soon part.
But first listen to my parting advice: although on account of your youth, no one may fear your efforts or
influence in my behalf, if you should remain here, yet
leave this castle as soon as you can, for fear you may
be insulted, or led into snares. Some of my faithful
servants will aid you in making your escape from this
place.

"Kunerick will take possession of the castle, and of
all it contains. Instead of being mistress of a castle,
having servants at your command, you will be poorer
than the humblest servant in our employ. But though
you be driven from your home, without being permitted to take with you any of the costly apparel and
jewels of your sainted mother, do not despair. Such
things are not of so much importance and value as to

deserve being mourned over. The possessions of this world are not, in the strictest sense of the term, ours; they are only lent us for a season; and you, by sad experience, will now learn how soon they may be taken away from us. And though we might be permitted to retain them as long as we live, death would at least deprive us of them. There are better treasures, of which no untoward circumstances in life, nor death itself, can rob us; and in comparison with which, gold, pearls, and jewels are nothing. I mean piety, industry, innocence, and humility. These, and other virtues, were the chief ornaments and the greatest riches of your dear mother; if you inherit these, they will in the end be better than riches.

"When you have escaped from the castle, endeavor to find the place where our faithful collier, honest Burkhard, lives. He, and his good wife, will take care of you, for my sake. There you can remain in quiet and safety, until he may find means to convey you to the castle of some of my friends. But, if you should be compelled, by force of circumstances, to spend years, nay, your whole life under his humble roof, always bear in mind, that we can live as contentedly, and die as happily in a cottage, as in the most splendid castle.

"Be not ashamed of rural employments. The marks of labor on the hand of the diligent are a greater honor, and deserve more respect than the glittering costly rings on the finger of the idle and dissolute. What a happy circumstance for you, my child, that your mother trained you up to habits of diligence, and taught you useful employments, rather than to seek your delight in costly apparel, in dainty viands, and in vain amusements.

"With constant diligence, unite fervent prayer. We are composed of body and soul. The powers of the body are to be employed in useful occupations. The soul is to be engaged in meditation and prayerful communion with God; the former procures bread for the body, the latter, nourishment for the soul. Always put your trust in the Lord; this will make your labor light and your rest sweet.

"Above all things, remain innocent and virtuous. Avoid those persons whose conversation is of such a character as to cause you to blush. I can no longer be present to take care of and counsel you. Remember the instructions of your dear mother, and ever act as though her spirit were hovering around you. Bear in mind that God sees all you do, and knows all your thoughts. Never do an evil act; never indulge a sinful thought.

"Grieve not on my account; pray for me, and then cast your care upon the Lord, for he careth for us. I know He will not forsake us. Your prayers shall not remain unanswered. As hard as my lot may be, the Lord can lighten it and make it supportable: bars and bolts cannot exclude him. He is everywhere, except in the heart of the wicked man. He will be with me in prison. Those that trust in God shall never be confounded.

"I firmly believe that God, in his own time, will rescue me from my bondage; but, if this should be the last time that you will see my face; if I should die in a loathsome prison, let me always have this consolation in my affliction—my Rosa has not forgotten the advice of her father; she is treading in the footsteps of her mother. And then, if in the dark, damp, dreary dungeon, my latter end shall arrive; if no eye of man shall witness my last struggle, nor ear of man hear my dying groan; and if no friendly hand shall be there to close my eyes in death, still I shall have this consolation—that I leave behind me a pious daughter, who, after she has accomplished her work in this world, will meet me and her mother in heaven.

"The parting advice of your sainted mother is now also mine. Remain virtuous and good. Love God. Cleave to your blessed Redeemer. Obey his kind instructions. Avoid the very appearance of evil. When you shall hear that death has loosed me from my chains, and freed me from my prison, then remember that the dying words of your mother were also my dying words. Follow this repeated dying counsel, and that God, who, for reasons to us unknown, so early removed your mother from our side, and who may also soon call me away, will unite us three again, to be separated no more.

"Here Rosa, this morning, I hung around my neck the golden medal which the emperor gave me, as a mark of honor and esteem. When our enemies came in upon us, I quickly hid it under my vest; I can scarcely look upon it without painful emotions. How fleeting and uncertain the honors of the world! In days past, the emperor honored me with this golden chain and medal, and now, like a criminal, I am bound with these iron chains.

"Take this mark of honor, as a keepsake from your father; part not with it, even in the greatest extremity;

after my death, it may be of the greatest importance
to you; by it you may, sometime or other, prove that
you are a descendant of a noble family—the family of
Linden castle.

"The emblems and mottoes engraven upon it are of
more value than the gold of which it is made.

"On one side, you see the eye of Omniscience, with
beautiful irradiations, and the motto, 'IF GOD BE FOR
US, WHO CAN BE AGAINST US?' Let this teach you that
God's watchul eye is ever upon us, and that those who
act as in his presence need fear no evil. On the other
side is a cross, with the inscription, 'THROUGH THIS I
CONQUER.' Let this put you in mind of the love of him
who died for us on the cross. In this world we have
many trials and sufferings; but through faith in a crucified Redeemer, and by a sincere obedience to his holy
commandments, a patient and faithful imitation of his
spotless example, in dependence upon his almighty
grace and a firm reliance upon his precious promises,
we shall be enabled to overcome every enemy, and
cheerfully to endure all that may be laid upon us.

"God has permitted a great affliction to come upon
us, but what is all that we can be called to suffer, when
compared with the sufferings through which the Saviour entered into his glory? Of his glory we shall be
made partakers, if we follow Him fully, fight the good
fight of faith, and patiently and submissively endure
the trial and afflictions allotted to us in life.

"And now, my dear daughter, listen to the last prayer
that you may ever hear from the lips of your father."
Rosa knelt by his side, whilst he offered up a most
fervent prayer, concluding with—"May God almighty

bless you, and the grace of our Lord Jesus Christ be with you always. Amen."

Once more her father kissed her, and said, "Rosa, I shall never forget you, nor cease to pray for you, but before I go, promise me that you will not forget your father's admonitions, and that you will constantly obey your mother's instructions."

"Oh! Every thing will I do that you and mother have told me—only suffer me not to leave you; I must go with you to prison and to death. Perhaps my entreaties and my tears may prevail with the hard-hearted Kunerick to let me accompany you, and wait upon you in prison."

A great noise was now again heard in the castle. Kunerick was collecting his men, and ordering them to prepare for their return home. A few were selected to remain to guard the castle. Armed men now rushed into Edelbert's chamber, and laid hold on him. Rosa clung firmly to his neck, and entreated them to take her also, but she was rudely torn away from him.

The soldiers led him down into the court, which was lighted up by pine torches. The gates were thrown open, and a number of mounted soldiers, each holding an additional horse, were in readiness. Kunerick's war-horse, elegantly caparisoned, stood chafing his silver bit, and pawing with his feet. Edelbert was thrown upon a crazy old cart, and two large wagons belonging to him were loaded with his goods, and his own horses taken from the stables and harnessed to them. Edelbert, not yet recovered from the effects of his wound, lay shivering in the open wagon, exposed to the rain and the cold. At last Kunerick threw himself upon his charger, ordered the bugle to be sounded, and they took up their line of march. Down the steep hill they went very slowly, and Rosa, who was following, easily overtook them. Kunerick was riding by the side of the cart which conveyed her father. Rosa, almost maddened by the idea of being separated from him, rushed between Kunerick's horse and the cart, and, raising her hands, begged that she might seat herself at her father's side, but no one regarded her. When they had reached the foot of the hill, Kunerick cried, "Onward, onward!" The horsemen put spurs to their horses, the drivers cracked their whips, and off they went at full speed. Rosa continued to follow them through the storm and rain until she was overcome by fatigue, and the murderous band was no longer to be seen or heard.

## Chapter Five.

### ROSA SEEKS REFUGE WITH
### THE HONEST COLLIER.

ROSA, who had seldom left the castle, and never without an attendant, now found herself alone upon the public highway, on a dark and stormy night. She knew not whither to go. She sought in vain for a shelter, where, protected from the rain, she might safely wait for the approach of day. At last she spied some young linden-trees whose tops overhung and sheltered a small spot of ground; here she sat down to pass the few remaining hours of the night. She felt no fear, for her mind was so engrossed with the scenes she had just passed through, that she thought of nothing else.

When the morning dawned, she came from her hiding-place, and looked around to see whether, by the surrounding objects, she could determine how far she had wandered from the castle. In the distance she saw, amidst the waving tops of linden-trees, the lofty towers of her home. The sight called up the most painful recollections of those happy days, now for ever gone; and she could not refrain from tears. "How I long," said she, "once more to see that home; perhaps I might still find there one of my father's faithful old servants, who would take compassion on me, and direct me to the house of Burkhard. That house in which I was born, in which I have enjoyed so much

happiness, is, I fear, closed against me for ever; for
scarcely had I passed through the gate, before it was
barred, and the drawbridge was raised to prevent my
return. My own sweet home is inhabited and guarded
by our most inveterate enemies, and it will not be safe
for me to venture near it. My father's advice to me
was, that I should go to honest Burkhard, the collier,
whom he once rescued from the cruel and hardhearted
Kunerick, and his advice shall be followed."

From what her father had related of the collier and
of his place of residence, she had learned, at least, in
what direction it was. Far in the forest, two mountains,
or rather high hills, raised their dark peaks; between
these was Burkhard's home. Rosa kept these hills
in view, and steered her course towards them. But
through the thick forest there was neither road nor
pathway. At one time she became entangled in the
underbrush; at another, she had to pass around some
marshy place, and ever and anon to seek a favorable
place to ford the mountain streams which crossed her
path. The density of the forest so obstructed her view,

that she could no longer see the mountain peaks which had served as her guides. Mid-day had arrived, yet no signs that she was approaching any human dwelling were visible. As she was passing along, all at once she heard a rustling noise in the bushes, but a few yards distant; and a noble buck, with tall, branching antlers, sprang up, and for a moment cast his large black eyes upon her, and then turned and fled. She had not gone much further, before she was frightened by the grunting of a fierce wild boar. He grinned most ferociously at her, and approached a few steps towards her. Rosa ran as fast as she could, afraid even to look behind her, till at last, quite out of breath, she stopped, and finding that he was not following her, seated herself upon a large stone, to take a little rest.

She had now entirely lost herself; she knew not which course to take, and the sun was about to set. "What shall I do?" cried she; "Must I pass the night in this dreary forest, in danger of being torn to pieces by wild beasts?"

Hunger, which, in consequence of excessive grief, she had not before experienced, was now so keenly felt, that she began almost to fear that she must suffer the horrors of starvation. But though well-nigh overcome by fatigue and want of food, she resolved to make one more effort to find her way out of the forest. Not far off she noticed a little cleared eminence; towards this she hastened, that she might have a more extended view. She ascended it; but nothing was to be seen but black, threatening clouds, hiding the last rays of the setting sun, and the wide forest, rendered more sombre by the coming shades of the evening. Rosa, almost despairing, fell upon her knees and began to pray—"My heavenly Father, thou hast said, 'Call upon me in the day of trouble and I will deliver thee, and thou shalt glorify me.' Oh! Verify this thy promise to me, a poor forsaken girl!" and while she was praying, the rays of the sun once more shone through the clouds, and beautifully gilded a rising column of smoke. "O my heavenly Father," exclaimed Rosa as she saw it, "thou has heard my prayer; thou hast fulfilled thy promise; praise and thanks are due to thy name; thou hast saved my life." "There," she said, "Burkhard must be burning coal; for no one lives in this whole forest but he." Animated with new life, she now hastened towards the place from which the smoke ascended.

Rosa was not disappointed; it was as she expected. Burkhard was burning coal there, and had already cleared a considerable spot in the woods. He was sitting upon a log near the burning coal-pit. Upon the stump of a tree he had fastened a square piece of board, which served him as a table, upon which was placed his supper of coarse bread, and butter, and an earthen jug with water. He was just singing a hymn of praise and thanksgiving to God before he partook of his evening meal. Rosa heard him at some distance, and, hastening her pace, was soon standing before him.

Burkhard, looking up, perceived a well-dressed young lady, and wondered how it was possible that a delicate female of her age should have ventured alone, to enter so dense and dangerous a forest; and most of all, that she should have been able to find him.

At first he did not recognise her; but as soon as he found it was the daughter of Edelbert, he rose, and

extending his hand, bade her welcome. "But how," said he, with the greatest astonishment, "how came you hither so late in the evening, and all alone? Surely my young lady must have lost herself. Well, well, so it is, you are here, and perhaps are hungry. I am keeping open house, in the midst of linden, pine, oak, and fir-trees. This is poor fare, indeed, for a young lady of rank, raised in a castle, but I have plenty of bread and butter and cheese. Come, take a seat beside me on my woodland sofa; hunger is a very good cook, and if you are hungry you will relish my supper. After you have refreshed yourself, and rested a little, you must then be accompanied home, or else, as sure as my name is Burkhard, your father will not sleep a minute this blessed night."

"My poor father!" replied she, bursting into tears and sobbing aloud; "Have you not yet heard what has happened to him?"

"Your father, the generous knight, to whom I owe my *all*!" cried he: (if his face had not been covered with smoke and coal, it would have been pale as death;) "Tell me, oh! Tell me instantly what has happened!"

"The Lord be gracious to him," replied Rosa, with a faltering voice; "Kunerick of Fichtenburg came upon us suddenly last night, took my father prisoner, loaded him with chains, and dragged him off to his castle."

"That evil one!" cried the collier, grasping his iron coal-rake, "May the devil—" but, recollecting himself, and letting his rake fall, he said, "I must not speak so; but he shall repent of this.—But how did this happen? Relate to me the circumstances. I cannot see how it is possible; it was only yesterday that I left the castle, and all was right. How could Kunerick take so strong a fortress in a single night?"

Rosa seated herself beside him, and began to relate the circumstances; but Burkhard soon noticed that, from exhaustion and want, she could scarcely speak. He therefore told her, first to eat and rest a little, and then proceed with the relation of the facts in the case. He ate but little himself, that there might be enough for Rosa. Having eaten nothing the whole day, her appetite was very keen. It was, as she said, the most delicious meal that she ever enjoyed—the coarse brown bread was so sweet, and the water from the mountain spring so refreshing.

"Yes, yes," said the collier, "hunger is the best of spices—a spice not to be bought by the rich, with all their wealth; but we poor people have it without paying for it! It is thus our God recompenses us for the many things of which we are deprived. We have but few cares, have good appetites, and can sleep soundly after our labor—blessings which the rich often do not possess!"

After Rosa had recovered from her fatigue, and thanked God for the food of which she had partaken, she related all the particulars of what had happened to them;--how her father was bound in chains, thrown upon a cart, and taken prisoner to Kunerick's castle. Burkhard listened attentively; but frequently interrupted her with expressions of contempt for such a hard-hearted wretch as Kunerick, and of compassion towards her father. When Rosa told him that her father had recommended her to his care, he was deeply affected by this mark of confidence.

"Well! Well! My young lady!" said he, brushing a tear from his eye, "God will not forsake his people in times of trouble. He will deliver Edelbert from this lion's den. From Him cometh affliction, from Him also deliverance. Let us rejoice that the Lord reigneth. He doeth all things well. Your father has intrusted you to my care! Well!—Look at yonder burning coal-pit; say but a word,—and for your sake, and for your father's sake, I would willingly jump into it. But now you require rest. It is too far for you to go to my house to-night, but I have a little hut here, such as we colliers build; there is just room enough in it for one person to sleep."

The hut was constructed of four poles driven into the ground obliquely, so as to meet at the top, interwoven with linden-twigs and covered with sods. "The four walls," jocosely remarked Burkhard, "have been forgotten in the building, and it is all roof. It is, however, so tight that not a drop of rain ever gets through it. The bed is made of the finest moss. A mat which I made of corn husks, serves the double purpose of a curtain for the bed, and a door for the hut. I assure you, however, that a person who is fatigued, and who possesses a good conscience, can sleep as soundly upon this as upon a bed of the softest down, surrounded by crimson curtains."

He now led the young lady into the hut, and then went and seated himself before his coal-pit, to watch the fire. During the whole night, he could think of nothing but the sad events which Rosa had related to him. The idea that the assistance which Edelbert had rendered him, in rescuing him from the power of Kunerick, was the chief cause of this calamity, occasioned him the greatest sorrow. He drew his sooty cap deep over his eyes, and for a time remained absorbed in meditation. At last, taking his cap between his folded hand, he prayed fervently that God would open a way of escape for the noble knight, and console Rosa in her affliction. He could not sleep for a moment. Rosa, however, soon fell into a profound slumber. She heard nothing of the rain nor the storm that raged during the night.

## Chapter Six.

### THE MEETING OF ROSA AND AGNES AT THE COLLIER'S HUT.

OWARDS morning, the storm ceased, the clouds were dispersed, and the sun rose in splendor and gilded the whole face of nature. The collier went from time to time and listened at the door of the hut, to learn if Rosa was yet awake. Several times he thought that he heard her move; but was glad to find her still asleep. "What a blessing," said he, "is sleep. It makes us forget our sorrows, and, for a season, removes the burdens which we are called to bear in life, and imparts renewed strength, that we may be better able to take them up again. My heavenly father," continued he, taking off his cap, "I thank thee for this, thy silent blessing. Thus must it also be with its kindred sleep—the longer sleep under the green covering of the grave; which perhaps is yet a greater blessing, for it frees us for ever from the cares and sorrows of life, and, if our day's work on earth be well done, it will be succeeded by a glorious awakening to an eternal day."

After a little while Agnes, the collier's daughter, a pleasant and good-natured girl, approached the hut, carrying a basket containing the breakfast, dinner, and supper of her father. She immediately perceived that something unusual had taken place; the countenance of her father indicated that his mind was greatly troubled. She inquired, "What has happened to you,

dear Father?" Fearful lest she might disturb the young
lady, he beckoned to her to be silent, and come to him.
He then told her what had befallen Edelbert and his
daughter, and that the young lady was now asleep
in the hut. Agnes was much affected, and wiped tear
after tear from her eyes.

In the mean time Rosa awoke. The rays of the rising
sun, which found their way through an opening that
the collier had purposely left in the hut, so as to have
a view of his coal-pit, shone directly in her face, and
roused her. At first, she knew not where she was; but
soon recollecting the scenes through which she had
passed the day before, she realized her situation, and,
bursting into tears, came to the door of the hut. The
collier and his daughter, as soon as they perceived her,
hastened towards her.

"In tears, dearest lady?" said the collier; "greet not
this delightful morning with tears. Behold how beautiful and clear the sky, after so dark and stormy a night;
how the dew-drop hang like glittering pearls upon the
leaves; how warm and pleasant the sun shines! So
shall the clouds and storms which now hang over you
and your father soon pass away. After a storm, the sun
always shines the brightest; and sorrow only prepares
us the better to relish the succeeding joys of life. Trust
only in the Lord, who guides the sunbeams and directs
the storm-wind."

Rosa and Agnes recognised, and greeted each other
most affectionately, as old acquaintances, though they
had not met for a long time.

Agnes now opened her basket, took from it an
earthen jug, and pouring out a bowlful of sweet milk,

placed it, together with bread and butter, upon the board that her father had fitted up for a table, and invited them to breakfast. Rosa seated herself upon the trunk of a tree, broke some bread into the bowl of milk, and with a wooden spoon, curiously carved, ate it, and also a piece of bread and butter, with the greatest relish.

After Rosa had eaten her breakfast, and expressed her gratitude to God and to the collier, the good man said to her: "Now, dear lady, go with Agnes to my house, and stay there until the Lord sends help. I must stay here for a while; in the mean time, I will consider, whether, with the help of God, I may not be able to do something for you and your father. As soon as my business will permit, I will join you at the house. Be not too much cast down, and weep not continually; this will not mend the matter; it will only injure yourself. Listen how sweetly the birds sing their morning hymns, as they cheerfully hop from branch to branch. Our heavenly Father provides for them, and they are happy. And will He not much more provide for you and your father? Therefore, you should trust in Him, and not yield to despondency. Agnes, be careful, and lead the young lady safely over the ledge of rocks, and along the mountain side. A good morning to your mother for me. Go now, children; the Lord be with you."

The path which they must take led through an almost impenetrable forest. For nearly an hour, they had to make their way among trees and bushes, without any path at all; then they passed between huge rocks covered with stunted trees and shaggy moss; following a narrow winding path, which led upwards along

the sides of the mountain. On one side, were high
perpendicular rocks, on other fearful ravines, so deep
that the tops of the tallest linden trees waved at their
feet. Rosa trembled as she looked down into the fearful depth, and then upon the narrow path before her.
"O Agnes!" exclaimed she, "Where are you leading
me to? I am afraid we shall never find our way out of
these dreary woods." Scarcely had the words escaped
her, when, on turning around a projecting rock, a most
beautiful little valley lay open to their view.

"Oh how beautiful!" exclaimed Rosa; "This is
indeed like coming out of the wilderness into the
promised land." She forgot, for a while, all her sorrows, and the thought that, perhaps, God would, in a
similar manner, unexpectedly open a way of escape
for her, and her father, from their present sorrows,
cheered her heart.

On a small eminence in the midst of this valley
stood Burkhard's house. It was built entirely of wood,
with a flat, projecting roof. On every side there was a
gentle declivity, and fruit trees of every variety, now
in full bloom, surrounded it; and a little brook, clear as
crystal, rolled on its murmuring course before the door.
The mountains which enclosed the valley sheltered it
from the bleak winds, so that vegetation was always
a few weeks earlier here than in the surrounding
country. On the meadows, several cows were quietly
grazing. On the mountain side, amidst the rocks, goats
were feeding on the tender bushes. In one corner of
a garden, filled with flowers and vegetables, was a
stand of beehives; and in the yard was a variety of the
finest fowls. Rosa entered the house, and being much

fatigued, sat down upon a pine bench. Every thing in the room was very plain, but neat and clean.

It was near noon when they reached the house. The collier's wife was busy in the kitchen; but as she heard her daughter speaking with some person, she entered the room. Imagining that Rosa had come to pay them a friendly visit, she bade her welcome in the most joyful manner. When, however, she was made acquainted with the circumstances which occasioned this unexpected pleasure, she was much affected. But soon composing herself, she endeavored, in the most affectionate manner, to comfort Rosa. "You are heartily welcome to our pleasant valley, and our quiet home. When your father built this house for us, he little thought that he was preparing a home for you; yet so mysterious and gracious are the ways of Providence, that He causes our acts of kindness to others, in many cases, to be the very means of blessing us in turn. Yes, yes, that passage of Scripture, 'He that watereth shall himself be watered,' is true in more than one sense. This property shall be yours; make yourself at home in your own house, until our heavenly Father shall re-store to you and your dear father your splendid castle, which, ere long, he will most certainly do. Meanwhile, let us all endeavor to live to his honor and glory."

Rosa replied with deep emotion, "How consoling it is, when, in our afflictions, we find such sympathy as this! I feel truly grateful for your kindness. What a happy circumstance for me, that my father was kind to you; God, through you, more than repays this kind-ness, in aiding his daughter."

The good woman was much at a loss how to treat

her guest in a manner becoming her rank in life. "Dear me!" said she, "We have a visit from a lady of rank and fortune, and I scarcely know what I shall give her for dinner. I have prepared nothing but some plain soup. If it only were not so late!—Yet, Agnes, do you keep the lady company, and I will try and prepare something better." Rosa endeavored, in vain, to set her mind at rest on this score. The woman went, and having prepared the best her means afforded, began again to make apologies, adding, "This is the first time in my life that I have had occasion to lament our poverty." "O my dear Gertrude," said Rosa, "you know not how rich and happy you are. Of your fare, in the enjoyment of which you are strong and healthy, and which tastes better to me than the richest dainties, I will not now speak. You have that which is far better—a quiet and happy home, and know little of the cares and anxieties, the noise and bustle of the world. In our castle, amidst all our splendor and wealth, we were continually harassed and perplexed—enemies were ever plotting our injury. My mother and I were in constant fear when father was away; and how dreadful the sudden calamity which, a few days ago, befel us! Oh, be thankful for this quiet and this peaceful abode, where, instead of the bustle of the world, the noise of rough soldiers, and the clangor of the war-trumpets, you hear the sweet songs of the birds—the lowing of your cattle, and the tinkling bells of your sportive goats. I would delight to spend my life in a place like this, if my father were only with me; and I am convinced that he would desire it as much as I."

# Chapter Seven.

## ROSA AS A COLLIER'S DAUGHTER.

O F honest Burkhard, his family had neither seen nor heard any thing for some days. He had told his daughter, when last she brought him his food, that she need not bring him any thing more, as he was going to town, and expected to be home in a few days. As he stayed rather longer than was anticipated, they had become very uneasy; but while they were talking about him one evening, he unexpectedly entered the house. He had a fine buck slung across his shoulder, and his bow and arrows in his hand. "How are you all?" said he, as he laid down his burden. "I trust you are more composed, my young lady." They were all very glad to see him, and his wife inquired, "Have you sold your coal well, Burkhard?" "Coal!" exclaimed he, with surprise; "I have been thinking little of selling coal. Alas! That my brightest hopes should have been turned to coals! I have been engaged in a business of which you little thought. I have visited several knights, whom Rosa's father assisted in distress, and called upon them to storm Kunerick's castle, and, by force of arms, release Edelbert; or to fall upon him when engaged in the chase, and keep him in confinement, until Edelbert should be released, and all his property restored. But all I could say was of no avail. They replied, that his castle was too well fortified, his force too strong, and that no attempt could be made until Edelbert's men returned from the wars; that then, perhaps, something might be done. Not one of them even as much as inquired after Rosa, the ungrateful fellows! I did not, therefore, my dear lady, mention your name to them, nor tell them that you were at my house; much less did I ask any of them to take you to their castles. It will be better for you to remain with us for the present."

"I would, a thousand times, rather stay with you," said Rosa, "if you would be so kind as to keep me."

"Keep you!" said Burkhard; "Do you think we have forgotten the kindness of your father; how he rescued me from the power of the cruel Kunerick—how he received me with my wife and child, for a while, into his house, and then gave me the home I now possess? I should be the most ungrateful wretch that ever lived. No! No! We have not become so unmindful of past favors. You can stay with us as long as you please. I will be a father to you, and my wife and Agnes will do every thing in their power to render the daughter of our benefactor comfortable and happy."

He now took the buck that he had shot, outside of the house, saying, "You have had but poor fare for some time, we shall soon have better; I will prepare something which Rosa's father was very fond of, and which I often prepared for him when we were out hunting."          On the following day, every possible arrangement was made for the accommodation of Rosa. The best room the house afforded was allotted to her. "Now," said Burkhard, when he had fixed every thing to his mind, "you have a comfortable room which you can call your own, and I will see to it that you shall have enough to eat. All the game in this vast forest belongs, of right, to your father, and you shall have venison, and ducks, and rabbits, and all kinds of wild game." In order to afford her new pleasures, and to divert her mind from her sorrow on account of her father, he would propose an evening's walk, and show Rosa his meadows, orchards, and beehives. He scarcely ever returned from the coal-pit without bringing something for her. At one time a basket of raspberries or blackberries; at another a string of trout from the mountain stream,—at another a number of mushrooms. When the weather was too unfavourable for him to go to his work, he entertained her with a recital of the many noble and generous deeds of her father, and the benevolence and charity of her pious mother, to which she always listened with no small degree of delight.

Burkhard's wife was determined not to be wanting in attention to the young lady. As she knew that Rosa, in her flight from the castle had brought no articles of clothing with her, save those she wore, she supplied her plentifully with some of her own manufacture.

Agnes also proved an affectionate and an agreeable companion for her. They were always together, both when engaged in some useful employment, and when enjoying a season of healthful recreation. Rosa instructed Agnes in needle-work and netting, and Agnes, in turn, instructed Rosa in domestic and rural employments. They went together to moisten the linen as it lay bleaching in the meadow—together they weeded the garden, and watered the flowers—together they climbed the mountain sides, and watched

the fish as they sported in the stream which watered
the valley; together they sat and listened to the songs
of birds which Rosa had learned to distinguish and
call by their various names;—together they picked
the ripe berries, and collected rare plants, which
Rosa had also learned to classify—and herbs, whose
medicinal virtues Agnes explained. Thus they spent
many a day, each striving to render the other happy.
Rosa, however, was not happy; the melancholy air of
her countenance plainly showed that her heart was ill
at ease. Her father's situation constantly preyed on
her mind. Often the family would miss her from the
house, and after a long search they would find her in
some secluded spot, upon bended knees, praying for
her father. The lapse of time, instead of healing the
wound, only served to make it still deeper. It was only
when they were consulting together, and devising
plans to rescue her father, or at least to mitigate his
sufferings, that her melancholy seemed to vanish, and
her countenance beamed with joy.

One Sunday, while at supper, the conversation, as
was often the case, was entirely engrossed with the
subject of her father's deliverance from prison. They
had nearly finished their frugal repast, while a dish
of delicious mushrooms remained untouched. "Eat!
Eat!" said Burkhard, "These are the best kind; and I
gathered them expressly for you. We care not much
for them, but they are considered a great rarity by the
rich and luxurious. I formerly brought a great many
to Linden castle. They are of a particular kind, and
grow in abundance near our coal-pits. A brother collier, whose coal-pits were on the domain of Kunerick,

also used to send of the same kind, by his children, to Forest castle. A daughter of his was also taken into the service by the steward of that castle. The wife of the steward, however, who is a real Tartar, turned off his daughter a few weeks ago: and my brother collier, who is none of the mildest of men, promised he would never send any more mushrooms to the castle. They might go and gather them for themselves, or do without."

Rosa leaped from her seat, and clapping her hands, exclaimed: "That is the very thing. I will clothe myself as a collier's daughter—carry mushrooms to the castle—seek to gain the confidence of the steward's wife—hire myself to her as a servant, and then, perhaps, I may manage matters so as to see my father; minister to his wants in some degree, and devise some method for his escape. O my Father in heaven," added she, raising her folded hands towards heaven, "aid me in carrying out this plan."

The honest collier shook his head, said "Hum! Hum!" and began to make objections, but Rosa promptly met them all. She hastened out of the room, and in a short time returned, dressed like a collier's daughter. She had changed her dress for that of Agnes. "How will this do?" said she; "Do I look like a collier-girl now?" "The clothes will do admirably," replied Agnes, "but your fair skin, and your delicate hands will soon betray you." Burkhard replied, "I can soon remedy that, if that is all!" He went out and brought a basin of water, into which he put a few berries, and told Rosa to wash her hands and face with it. She did so, and Agnes and her mother exclaimed, "That will do, that will do, no one will suspect you now."

Rosa determined to lose no time, and prepared to start for the castle the next day; for she was afraid that if she delayed, the steward's wife might obtain a servant, in the place of the one who had left. "If you will go," said Burkhard, "make the attempt in dependence upon the Lord. This very evening, I will go and gather the finest mushrooms which can be found; and to-morrow, Agnes will accompany you through the forest, as far as the top of a hill on the main road, from which the castle can be distinctly seen. Then, Agnes will wait until you return."

Early on the following morning, Rosa was ready to start. She took the basket of mushrooms on her arm, and Agnes carried another with some eatables. The collier and his wife gave her some useful instructions, and, imploring many blessings upon her, bade her go in God's name. "The good child," said he, brushing the tears from his eyes, "will succeed; for the promise which God has given to them that honor father and mother, cannot fail."

## Chapter Eight.

ROSA SEEKING EMPLOYMENT
AT THE ENEMY'S CASTLE.

 OSA, in company with Agnes, soon reached the end of the forest, which for a time had separated her from the busy world. The castle, with its lofty watch-tower, was now in view. But as she gazed upon it, she began to tremble, and her mind was agitated by a variety of distressing reflections. "Oh!" said she, "perhaps in the darkest dungeon of that castle, lies my father—does he yet live? Is he well? Or have sorrow and misery put an end to his existence? If he yet lives, shall I ever see him, and minister to his wants? O God, do thou direct my steps, and let me find favor with the people to whom I am now going."

Rosa now parted with Agnes, and pursued her journey alone. As she drew near the castle, she found the gate thrown wide open, and saw Kunerick, mounted upon his bold, spirited charger. He was splendidly dressed, and his long white plume waved sportively in the breeze. Surrounded by servants and huntsmen, all mounted, he was just ready to start on a hunting expedition. The sight almost overpowered Rosa; her knees trembled, and she would have fallen, had she not seated herself upon a bench at the gate. The huntsman's horn now gave the signal for their departure, and, in a few minutes, Kunerick and his party were out of sight.

GILBERT & GIHON.

Rosa felt almost unable to rise; nor did she rightly
know what course to take—whether to go in at once,
or wait until some of the servants passing by should
invite her to enter. Whilst she sat thus, thinking what
to do, several children approached the gate. Rosa,
seeing they were a little timid, bid them a good day,
and asked them their names. Thus encouraged, they
came and seated themselves beside her. Othmar, after
a little time, lifted the lid of her basket to see what was

in it; whilst his little sister Bertha reached for some
wild flowers which Rosa had plucked in the woods
and fixed in her bonnet. Rosa gave her the flowers;
and she gave to each of the children, also, a few of
the early pears which the collier's wife had placed in
her basket.

The children belonged to the steward of the
castle, who was looking out of the window, and
observing Rosa attentively. He was pleased to see
that she took so much notice of them. The correct
language, the sweet voice, the pleasing manner, and
the neat and clean dress of the country girl, made a
favorable impression upon him. "In my life," said
he, "I have never seen a peasant's daughter like her;
her parents must be most excellent people, and they
must have taken great pains with her."

He came out and invited her to go into the house.
"What have you for sale?" said he, in a friendly
manner. Rosa opened her basket, and showed him
her mushrooms. "How much do you ask for them?"
"Whatever you are willing to give," said she; "for I
trust you will not give a poor girl too little." "That
is well said," replied he; "tarry awhile, I will take
them to the castle, and will bargain for you; it is a
long time since any mushrooms have been brought
here for sale." Taking up the basket, he remarked,
as he was going out of the door, "I'll guaranty you
shall not receive too little for them."

The steward had scarcely left the room, when his
wife entered. "How did you get in here, you bold
jade?" said she to Rosa. "Who are you? What do you

want? How dare you come into my house without being asked? This instant clear out, or I'll throw this dish at your head, and set the dogs on you."

The children interceded for Rosa, and showed the pears and flowers she had given them; and the steward now entered with the empty basket, and the money for the mushrooms.

"Now, now, wife," said he, "what's the matter again? you are always so hasty. This appears to be a modest and good girl, and I was just thinking, that, as we need a servant, she would suit us, and would perhaps be willing to come; but you are so quick and irritable, that I am afraid no one will stay with you, as a servant. The girl did not come in without being invited; I told her to come in."

"That alters the matter," replied she; "as you told her to come in, she may stay." "You must not take it ill," said she, addressing Rosa, "that I got a little warm, for, together with the office of steward, my husband is gatekeeper, and we must be cautious whom we permit to enter in these days."

"You are right," said Rosa; "you did not know that any person invited me to come in, and it looked quite suspicious to find me, a stranger, alone in your house. I respect your fidelity and zeal, and beg your pardon."

This reply entirely satisfied the woman; for she was one of that numerous class, with whom it is impossible to get along, unless you let them have their own way. "Well, as you have shared your pears and flowers with my children," said she to Rosa, "you shall share our dinner with us. Come, sit down at the table, and eat."

Rosa obeyed, but the children asked her so many

questions, that she scarcely found time to eat. She, however, replied to all their questions in so mild and affectionate a manner, that she gained the confidence and esteem of their mother.

When Rosa took her basket and prepared to go, the children cried, "Stay here, stay here always."

"Yes," said the mother, "I would be much pleased to have you stay. Would you not like to come and live with me as a servant?"

"With all my heart," rejoined Rosa, "and I would try and serve you honestly and faithfully."

"Very well," said the steward's wife, "but first go home and speak to your parents, and if they have no objections, you can come on next Saturday."

The woman told Rosa what wages she would give her; and putting a few little articles into her basket, said, "Go and take these things to your parents, as a salutation from your new mistress, and may you reach your home safely."

Rosa thanked her heartily, and hastened towards the place where she had left Agnes. Agnes had all this time been sitting under a shady tree, knitting, and waiting patiently for Rosa. No sooner did she see Rosa coming, than she ran to meet her. "I am glad you have come," said she, "you must be tired and hungry; come, sit down with me under the shade of yonder tree, where my basket is; and eat a piece of pie, and take a drink of milk, and tell me what success you have met with."

"Dear me!" said Rosa, as Agnes opened the basket of provisions, with which her mother had supplied them, "You have not tasted any thing since I left you.

Why did you not eat? I have eaten my dinner, do you eat. I will sit down with you, while you are eating, and rest myself a little. We must not, however, delay long, lest the night overtake us in the forest. I can relate my adventures while we are walking, and also take a piece of pie and eat it on the road." "So can I," replied Agnes; "let us go."

Far in the forest, when the sun had already been for some time hid behind the hills, Burkhard and his wife, who had begun to feel uneasy about them, met them. They were glad to see the girls in good spirits, and more particularly so, to hear that, so far, the undertaking had succeeded admirably. With light hearts, and engaged in pleasant conversation, they quickly passed over the remaining part of their way. As they reached the valley, the full moon, which had risen in splendor, shed her silver light upon the peaceful home of these good people. Rosa, though much fatigued, felt peculiarly happy. She retired to her chamber at an early hour, and ere she laid down to sleep, thanked God, that he had thus far blessed her arduous and difficult undertaking, and fervently implored Him to aid her in its final accomplishment.

## Chapter Nine.

## ROSA IN THE CAPACITY OF A SERVANT.

HE next Saturday, on which Rosa left, was a sorrowful one for them all. Rosa found it no easy task to tear herself away from these good people, who manifested so deep an interest in her welfare, and to exchange her happy and peaceful abode for the fortress of an enemy, of whom she could never think without terror. She knew, moreover, that in a situation so new to her, and in the performance of labor to which she was so little accustomed, many and severe trials awaited her. Yet in reliance upon God, and from love to her dear father, she did not shrink from the task, but entered upon it with delight. Honest Burkhard and his wife accompanied her some part of the way, and then, with their best wishes, and fervent prayers, took leave of her. Agnes, however, accompanied her the whole distance, and aided her in carrying a small bundle of clothes.

The wife of the steward received them kindly. "You are a good girl," said she to Rosa, "to keep your promise: come in, girls, and I will get you something to eat." Rosa opened her basket and handed the woman a small present, which Gertrude had sent in return for the one she had received from her; and also gave the children some pears, apples, and nuts. This pleased them very much, and at once raised Rosa in the estimation of both the mother and the children.

After dinner, Agnes, with many tears and sighs, took leave of Rosa.

"Now, now," said the woman, "don't cry so, you can come and see your sister often; I shall always be glad to see you; and if you will supply us with some of your excellent mushrooms, I shall be still better pleased, and I will pay you for them into the bargain. After Agnes had gone, Rosa, separated from all her friends, and in the fortress of her father's bitterest enemy, felt herself forsaken by all but her God.

Agnes had not been gone long, when the woman called Rosa, and said, "Girl, come here, I have something to tell you. Now listen attentively to what I say."

"I know that people say, that I am so quick tempered and cross, that no girl can live with me, and that, in the course of five years, I have had twenty-five different servants. This is reported through the whole neighbourhood. But people say nothing about the character of the girls that I had in my employ, nor of the many faults which they had. I will therefore tell you what kind of girls they were."

She now began with great warmth, and in a most loquacious manner, to give the character of her former servants.

"There was Bridget,—but I will not mention the names of the girls, lest I should ruin their characters. I only want to tell you of their faults as a caution to you. Well, there was Bridge—she was proud, and always professed to know how to do things better than myself. Once I set her to baking cakes, and she left them to burn, almost as black as coals; and then was so bold as to tell me to my face, that the cakes were not burnt, but were just as they ought to be. This I could not endure. I got angry, and told her to go. The next was Sal: she was never contented—sour, fretful, and peevish, and found fault with her victuals. More than a dozen times, she complained that she had too much work to do, and got too little wages. Well, I could put up with it no longer, and told her to go and hunt a place where she would get better wages, and have less to do."

"The third was too lazy to live. I thought she would never get through with her work. She was too lazy to stoop. When she had swept the rooms, she would let the broom lie in a corner, and stumble over it half-a-dozen times before she would pick it up. Every morning I had to call her, ten times at least, before she would get out of her bed. I believe if I had not wakened her, she would have been sleeping yet. Who could put up with such a girl? At last I told her to be off, and declared, if she was too lazy to go, I would get one of the men to bring a cart and haul her away."

"The fourth was thievish: butter, cream, and meat,

she used to steal like a cat. One morning, in spring, I was going to meet my husband, who had been absent for a few days, and was expected to return that morning. I had gone but a short distance, when, on looking back, I perceived a great smoke coming out of the kitchen chimney. I immediately returned, and lo! When I entered the kitchen, there was Kate, baking apple-flitters for herself. That was too much for me, as you may well suppose. I got angry, and packed her off in an instant. Who could bear such a girl as that?"

"The fifth was slovenly and dirty. True, on Sundays and holidays she was dressed in style; but during the week, while at her work, she was so ragged and dirty that she looked like a scarecrow. I believe if she had been stuffed and hung up in the fields, she would not only have scared away the crows, but even the wild hogs. One day, the knight saw her, and told my husband we must send her off; it was a disgrace to his castle to have such a person about; so Mag had to go."

"The sixth was a thoughtless, heedless, good-for-nothing girl. She never attended to what I said to her. I had to tell her everything she had to do, and repeat it at least half-a-dozen times. She broke more dishes, cups, and glasses, than there are days in the year. The spoons, she often threw out with the dish-water; and one day I found one in the stable, which the hogs had champed almost to pieces. Not long after, she broke a large glass. I heard the crash, and ran into the kitchen. She, however, had already gathered and hid the pieces, and denied having broken any thing. I looked for the pieces, but could not find any. At last I thrust

my hand quickly—for I was angry—into a large tub
of water, and cut my finger most severely with some
of the glass. This vexed me still more, and I said, 'Sus,
you'll break no more glasses for me; make up your
bundle, and go.'"

"The seventh was a real tattler. She repeated every
thing she heard. She was always listening at the key-
hole, and would tell every thing that was said, and
thus create frequent difficulties between us and our
neighbours. If you wished to have any thing made
public, you needed only to tell Ursel, and you might
be sure it would soon be known, far and near. She
was—but listen! The bell is ringing, some one is at the
gate, and I must go. I will tell you more about them
another time. To-morrow is Sunday, and then we shall
have time to talk. Bear in mind their faults, and shun
them; and then I trust we shall get along very well
together."

Rosa at once saw the character of the woman, who,
for a season, was to be her mistress; and only mildly
remarked, that "if a servant had the tenth part of the
faults she had mentioned, she deserved blame; and
that a good house-keeper, who desired to have things
done as they should be, could not be satisfied with her.
I shall endeavor to avoid their errors, and do my best
to serve you."

Rosa was, indeed, a pattern of a good servant. She
served her mistress according to the rule laid down by
Christ and his apostles: "Not with eye-service as men
pleasers: but as the servant of Christ, doing the will
of God from the heart." She was always industrious,
and it was a pleasure to see how well and quickly

she performed her work. She never had to be told the second time to do a thing. She had learned from her mother to do things at the proper time, and to do them well: therefore she never had to be told to attend to the ordinary, and every-day duties of the household; these were done before any one had occasion to remind her of them. She was cleanly about her person and her work; she suffered nothing to go to waste; the secrets of the family she kept inviolate; the interests, happiness, and prosperity of the family, she made her own; she always appeared contented and happy; and if she made a mistake, she was always ready to ask pardon. And when her mistress was out of humor, and scolded her without cause, she knew the great art of being silent at the proper time; and her silence, and mild, unruffled countenance had a greater effect than any thing she could have said, to appease the woman's anger. Rosa's conduct had a great influence upon the disposition of her mistress, and, to the no small astonishment of her husband, many a day passed, without her giving way to her naturally violent temper.

Rosa had, however, a hard time of it. She was well able to discharge all the duties and offices suited to her rank and station in life; but unaccustomed as she was to the laborious duties she now had to perform, she found them almost beyond her strength, and very unpleasant. She was compelled to rise before day, every morning, to carry wood and water into the kitchen, kindle the fire, wash the dishes, scrub the floor, and perform many similar duties. As she had never before done some of these things, it may easily be imagined, that, at first, she went awkwardly to work, and had to submit to be called stupid, dumb, and awkward. Her food was, indeed, good and substantial, but yet it was very different from what she had been accustomed to, and many times it was with no small degree of effort, that she could partake of it.

When she had toiled from morning until night, and, after all her endeavors to please, was taunted and scolded by her mistress, she would retire to her chamber, weary and disheartened. Her only refuge was her Saviour, and her God; to Him she fled, and told her tale of woe, asking for grace, and seeking his direction. "I am willing to endure all," said she, "if only in the end I shall be able to see my father, and mitigate his sufferings, or release him from his prison."

## Chapter Ten.

ROSA VISITS HER FATHER IN PRISON.

OSA had now been at service for some time, and had endured many hardships, but no opportunity of seeing her father had yet presented itself. It was extremely trying for her to think of being so near him, and yet not be able to see him. From the very first, however, a ray of hope was kindled in her bosom. She observed, that the steward had charge of the prisoners, and daily carried them their food. And by inquiring after them, she ascertained that her father was yet alive and well. Frequently, she asked the steward to show her the prisoners; but he shook his head, and told her she had no business there. When she saw the steward taking the black bread, and the jug of water, to the prisoners, she could scarcely contain herself; and often said, "My sufferings are nothing compared with those of my father. I will endeavor to bear all with resignation to the will of heaven."

One evening, as the steward was preparing to give the prisoners their food, he said to Rosa, "Rosa, you must come along with me; I want to show you the prisoners, for to-morrow I must accompany the knight on a journey, and then you will have to attend to them. My wife has little time, and no inclination, for such work." He took a basket in one hand, and a bunch of keys in the other, while Rosa carried the earthen jug, full of water. This was altogether unexpected to her; she could hardly realize that in a few moments she would see her father. And great as was her joy, she yet felt a kind of fear. She trembled in every limb, and followed the steward with a palpitating heart, through the long dark passage. She endeavored to compose herself, as much as possible, and resolved so to conduct herself as to leave no room for suspicion: for she knew that if, at the sight of her father, she should manifest any extraordinary emotion, suspicion would at once be excited, and the keys of the prison would not be intrusted to her.

The steward halted at a little opening in the wall, closed with a shutter, which he unlocked. Rosa tremblingly peeped in, and saw a man with a long beard, and long uncombed hair, whose countenance seemed marked with wild despair. "This man," said the steward, "was once a brave and noble warrior, but through gambling and drinking he was led astray and became a highway robber. I should not like to share his reward." The steward then gave him his bread and water, locked the shutter, and passed on.

He opened another shutter, and Rosa saw a pale, haggard female, with dishevelled hair and sad countenance, bound with chains. "This person," said he, as he reached her the bread and water, "was one of the handsomest young women I ever knew. She is accused of murdering her child. By no means must you ever open the door of her prison; despair has rendered her wild and furious!"

"But to this man," said the steward, as he was unlocking the iron-grated door of another cell, "to this man we may safely go; he is a good man, mild and patient as a lamb. It is the brave knight Edelbert of Linden castle."

Rosa would never have recognised him. He was so pale and emaciated, his beard so long and bushy, and his clothes so discolored and torn. He sat upon a stone seat, to which he was fastened with a long chain, which permitted him to walk about in his cell. The table before him was also of stone, and upon it stood a pitcher of water, and beside this lay a piece of coarse, hard bread. The good knight rested his head upon his left hand, and the right hand he extended to his keeper. An old bedstead, with some straw and a single blanket, stood in the corner. This cell was larger than the rest, being designed for persons from the higher ranks in life. Its walls and high arches were gray with age. It had a small window with strong iron grates to admit the light, but the glass was so covered with smoke and dust, that the little light which shone through it, only served to cast a most sombre shade over the dreary place.

"Knight," said the keeper, "to-morrow my servant-girl will attend to you, as I shall be absent a few days."

Edelbert looked at Rosa, and though he did not know her, was nevertheless forcibly reminded of his daughter. "Ah!' said he, heaving a loud sigh, "of this age and size was my daughter. Steward, have you received no intelligence of her? Where she is, and what she is doing? I have besought you a hundred times to try and obtain some information concerning her."

The steward replied, "God only knows where she is! I have inquired of hundreds, and no one knows any thing of her."

"Is it possible! Can not one be found, of all those knights who professed to be my friends in the days of my prosperity, to take compassion upon a poor, lonely, child?" He thought indeed of honest Burkhard, and hoped she might be with him; but he was afraid to mention his name, for fear Kunerick would search after him and make him as unhappy and miserable as he was himself. "Well!" said he, "I indulge the hope that she is with some good and pious persons, who will take care of her. O my dear sir, you cannot imagine how affectionate and kind my Rosa was; it was her delight to render me happy." Addressing himself to Rosa, he said, "If your parents are yet living, be as kind, obedient, and affectionate to them as my child was to me, and you will be rewarded for it."

Rosa wellnigh lost command of herself; she wept, and cried aloud, and was several times upon the very point of throwing herself upon her father's neck.

Edelbert was surprised to see the girl so much affected, and said—"You have, perhaps, lately lost your father or mother, as you weep so much."

Rosa could scarcely speak, but sobbingly replied, "My mother died many years ago, my father is still living, but is in great distress."

"You have a tender heart; may the Lord preserve you from the temptations of the world, and have mercy upon your father."

"True," replied the steward, "you have almost too tender a heart to discharge these duties for me; you must muster up courage, and not weep so, or else you cannot attend to the prisoners in my absence."

"She is a good girl," continued he, addressing himself to Edelbert—"so cleanly and diligent, so mild and amiable, that, in a circle of ten miles round, you cannot find her equal. I shall never be able to repay her for what she has done for my children. If my Bertha grows up to be like her, I shall be truly thankful."

"God bless you, my child," said Edelbert, reaching to her his fettered hand. "Continue to be virtuous and good; pray fervently, and trust in the Lord, and God will surely help your father, and bless him for your sake."

"God grant it," said Rosa, and raising his hand to her lips, kissed it.

It was high time that the steward should take his departure, as Rosa could not have contained herself much longer. It was with great difficulty that she walked through the dark passage, and would several times have fallen, had she not held herself up, and been supported by the side of the rough wall.

## Chapter Eleven.

### ROSA MAKES HERSELF
### KNOWN TO HER FATHER.

HE remaining part of the evening, Rosa felt very sad. The condition of her father, his pale and haggard visage, his gloomy cell, were continually before her mind, and nothing sustained her but the idea that she would soon be able to make herself known to him, and render his situation a little more comfortable.

After her necessary work was finished, she retired to her chamber, fell upon her knees, and fervently prayed that God, who had so far blessed her undertaking, would aid her in the future, and enable her to prove a comfort and blessing to her dear father. She now laid down upon her bed, but did not fall asleep until near midnight.

At one o'clock, her mistress called her to prepare breakfast for her husband, who intended to leave the next hour. The steward praised Rosa's breakfast, and promised, if she attended faithfully to the duties he had assigned her, that he would bring her a present. After this, he mounted his horse and departed. Her mistress again retired to rest, and all was quiet. Rosa now took the key of her father's cell, which she had observed was larger and stronger than the rest, and the lantern of the steward, which hung on the same nail with the keys, put a small lamp into it, and hastened to the

prison. She cautiously unlocked the bolted and barred door, and found her father sitting, with folded arms, upon the seat where she left him in the evening.

He was much surprised to perceive, by the faint light of the lamp, that it was the same girl who had been there with the steward in the evening.

"Is that you, my child?" said he, "So late at night, or rather so early in the morning; for I have just heard the watchman cry two o'clock."

"Forgive me," said she, in a low tone of voice, "that I disturb you; but I perceive you have slept as little as I have. I want to speak with you alone; therefore I come at this unseasonable hour, so that we may not be overheard."

"Child," replied Edelbert, "this is a dangerous business for you. It might be productive of evil consequences. A young girl, like you, ought never to be out at this hour of the night."

"Fear not for me," said Rosa; "all is quiet and at rest without, except the watchman. I have weighted this matter well, and prayed much over it. God directed my steps hither, and I know He is with me. I have, at present, only a few words to speak to you. The deep concern you manifested about your daughter affected me so much that I could not sleep; and I have come to bring you some intelligence concerning her."

"Intelligence concerning my Rosa!" said he, in haste. "Oh! If this be so, then you are as welcome to my cell as an angel from heaven. Delay not!—Speak, speak! Do you know her? Have you seen her? Is she well? Keep me not in suspense!"

"I can give you certain and correct information of her," said Rosa. "Look here, do you know this chain, and this golden medal?"

"Is it possible? Let me see; yes, it is the same. This chain and golden medal I gave to my daughter, on the night in which I was separated from her. But how did you get possession of it? I charged her never, upon any condition, to part with it. You must be very intimate with her, and perhaps she has only intrusted it to you, in order that I may the more readily believe that the intelligence you bring concerning her is true."

"She never parted with it—dearest Father, I am Rosa!"

"You!" cried Edelbert; "Deceive me not; my daughter was fair, as the flower whose name she bears."

"Father," said she, "it was necessary for me, in order to avoid suspicion, to change the hue of my countenance, as well as my dress; and honest Burkhard has given me a simple and harmless wash, which I occasionally use for this purpose. Look at me, father; see the mole on my neck!"

"O my Rosa! My own child! Come into my arms. I know that you yet live, that you are near me, and, above all, that you are virtuous and good, and have not forgotten the instructions of your dearest mother and your affectionate father. Now I can die in peace. I can now be happy in my dungeon."

Rosa hung upon his neck, and could only articulate, "My dearest, dearest father!"

"But tell me, my child, how came you hither? Reveal to me this mystery. By what untoward circumstances have you been brought so low, as to be forced to become the servant of the lowest officer of this castle?"

Rosa told her father briefly her whole history—how kindly she was received by the collier and his family; how she formed her plan of hiring herself to the steward of the castle,—for no other purpose than to have an opportunity of seeing him, and ministering in some humble measure to his wants. "And now," said she, "God has fulfilled my heart's best desire. He has afforded me this opportunity of embracing my dearest father once more, and perhaps of doing something for him. Oh! I am the happiest of daughters; my whole life shall be devoted to Him, who, in his kind providence, has so far blessed my endeavors to see you."

"Say not, my child," said her father, weeping, "the happiest of daughters, but the best of daughters you certainly are—and I am now the happiest of fathers. How often have I been pained to think that I was forced to exchange this golden chain for these chains of iron! But now, O my heavenly Father, I thank Thee for this mysterious providence! Had it not been for this affliction, I never should have enjoyed this proof of my daughter's ardent affection, and her self-denying exertions in my behalf. I felt proud when the emperor placed this golden chain around my neck, as a token of his regard, but I feel prouder and happier now, with this iron chain, which has long been galling my wrist. I would not exchange the emotions which now swell my bosom for all the riches of the world. What, in comparison with this feeling, is the value of this medal and chain? Yet the medal has its worth; it is of value, not because it is of the purest gold, but because it bears mottos and inscriptions upon it, which have now been verified in our experience.

"Yes, dearest Rosa, now we learn that the eye of God has watched over you. He has taken care of you, preserved you from temptation and sin, and brought you, virtuous and happy, into my arms. He, whom walls, and bolts, and prison-doors cannot exclude from His people, has looked in mercy into my cell and afforded me this happiest hour. God is with us. Kunerick meant it for evil, but God only made him the instrument of affording us the purest, the most heavenly delight. Through crosses and afflictions, God leads to happiness and bliss. The truth of this we now experience, and I firmly believe we shall yet experience it more fully in days to come. Kunerick, amidst his midnight carousals, his music, his wine, and the dance, may consider me the most miserable of beings; but let the noise of their mirth and revelry reach my cell, at the midnight hour, as it often has done; I am happier in my cell, with bread and water, than he is in his gorgeous palace, with the most delicious fare. The chain has never been forged, which can bind the freeborn spirit and hinder it in its flights heavenward, or restrain it from holding communion with the Friend of sinners.

"My dear Rosa, it has been good for you, thus early, to be taught in the school of affliction and sorrow. It has led you to choose rather to spend the hours of midnight in prison with your father, than to enjoy the pleasures of sin. Through afflictions we are preserved from the allurements of vice, and kept close to the Saviour. O Rosa! Rosa! Ever keep near to the Lord; obey all the commandments, as you have kept that, which says, 'Honor thy father and thy mother.' Conquer, through faith in a crucified Redeemer, the temptations of the world, and of sin; despise the false pleasures of this world, and patiently endure the trials of life, and you will be happier than the prince upon his throne."

Rosa now bade her father farewell; and darkening her lamp by hiding it under her apron, she hastened to her room to take her rest, just as the watchman had cried his last hour.

## Chapter Twelve.

ROSA MINISTERS TO HER FATHER IN PRISON.

OSA had scarcely sat down to breakfast with her mistress and the children, when Kunerick unexpectedly entered, and appeared very much agitated. Rosa trembled exceedingly. She had never seen him enter the steward's house since she had been at service there, and could conceive of nothing else, but that she had been seen entering the prison, and was betrayed. Kunerick said in a loud and harsh voice: "For some time you shall not be needed at the gate. I have given it in charge of four soldiers. Both of you, instantly repair to the kitchen of the castle, and lend a helping hand; for, to-day, or to-morrow, I expect to entertain some noble guests." Rosa's fear began to subside, and she breathed more freely. Kunerick had, indeed, observed her alarm, and the paleness of her countenance, but he imagined that she was only awed by his presence; and he felt that he was a man of greater importance than ever, when he reflected that his very presence inspired even the servants with awe and reverence. Rosa accompanied her mistress to attend to the work assigned them. At noon, a neighbouring knight, with a numerous retinue, arrived; and on the next day, another, accompanied with a still more numerous suite, and besides these, a great number of persons, some on horseback, and others on foot, arrived every hour. Not only was the castle itself, in which the knight resided, full of soldiers and officers, but also all the buildings in the spacious court which surrounded it. Large fires were kindled, and they cooked and ate, and made a great noise. Rosa wondered what all this could mean. Late in the evening, when Rosa was giving the children their supper, her mistress came in, and raised her hands, and exclaimed almost out of breath, "O children, children, there is to be war, and your father, who was out, calling the soldiers together, has just returned, and must also accompany them. To-morrow, at the dawn of day, they start."

On the following morning, the war-trumpet gave the signal to prepare for the march. The steward, who was one of Kunerick's bravest soldiers, buckled on his armor, and, fully equipped for war, bade adieu to his wife and children. "Pray for me," said he, "my wife and children, and you also, my good Rosa, that I may be preserved from danger, and may return in safety among you again."

The soldiers were now formed into companies, by their officers; and then ordered to their places in the line by the commander-in-chief of the whole force. They presented quite a martial and imposing appearance, as they marched through the gate into the main road. Kunerick was the last to leave. When all had passed through the gate, he gave the keys to the old bailif, saying, "Here, thou old, faithful servant, take these keys; keep them in your possession day and night. You will suffer no one to pass in at the gate, unless you, and at least two of the soldiers whom I have left to guard the castle, are present; this you will attend to at the peril of your life." He then gave his horse the spurs, and soon joined the army. As soon as he was gone, the drawbridge was raised, and the gates closed, and well secured.

Rosa and her mistress had to assist at the castle during the whole of that day, in putting things in order again. In the evening, her mistress said to her, "Rosa, to-morrow I intend to visit my mother, and I shall take the children with me. The tumult and noise of the soldiers, and the departure of my husband, has quite unnerved me; perhaps a little excursion will be of some service. I shall not be at home until late in the evening. As you, also, must be tired by yesterday's labor, you may rest yourself to-day. The knight has intrusted the keeping of the gate to other hands, so you need not be concerned about that; but don't forget to attend to the prisoners and give them their food." So, early in the morning, she took the children and departed.

No one could be happier than Rosa. For some days, she had been so much engaged, that she could spend but a few moments with her father; but now, as she had nothing to do, she could spend nearly the whole day in his cell. Ever since she first saw her father in prison, she had been devising plans to render him more comfortable. During her leisure moments, and after she had retired to her chamber, she was often employed until midnight in making a shirt for him, out of some of the linen that she and Agnes had bleached in the meadow, and which Burkhard's wife had given her. The favorable opportunity which now offered itself, she diligently improved. She went to the prison, taking with her the linen she had prepared, and a bowl of water, some soap, and a towel; gave her father the keys to unlock his chains, and retired. When Rosa returned, after the lapse of an hour, he said, "I feel like another man; such a luxury I have not enjoyed for a long time. I have not had a change of linen for weeks, nor any soap since I came to prison; nor have my chains been removed from my galled wrists and ankles."

"Now, Father," said Rosa, "you must enjoy a little of God's pure and fresh air." From the dark passage which led to the cells, there was a door which opened into a small garden, enclosed by a high wall. This was allotted the steward, for the cultivation of vegetables, and Rosa had it in charge. Into this garden Rosa led her father. It was a beautiful and pleasant morning. The sun shone in all its splendor, and there was a most delightful and refreshing breeze. The good knight, in coming out of his dungeon into the open air, felt as though he were in a new world. "Ah!" said he, "If such be the bliss I now feel, in exchanging my dungeon for this garden, what must not the soul experience when death releases it from all its afflictions and sorrows on earth, and ushers it into the garden above,—the paradise of God!"

Rosa now brought her father his breakfast. Instead of his coarse bread and water, she gave him some meat, a little broth, and some bread and butter, and placed them on a bench under the shade of a large tree. She told him that he might spend the whole day there, if he chose. "Most cheerfully would I," added she, "stay with you, but I have to attend to some little matters for my mistress; I will, however, come and see you frequently."

After she was gone, Edelbert walked up and down in the garden, to enjoy the benefit of exercise, and the influence of the sun and air. His whole system was invigorated, and he blessed God for these mercies, and especially also for the affection of his daughter. "Love," said he, "is the sun in the world of mind, which warms, enlivens, and cheers the heart. Without love and affection, this world would be dark and cheerless as my dungeon."

Rosa, who had also brought her father something nice for dinner, and visited him many times during the day, came in the evening to lead him to his prison, and, with her own hands, to put on his heavy irons,—a duty from which she almost shrunk in despair. But how great was his astonishment when he entered his cell! He at first thought she had made a mistake, and taken him into a different room, so great was the change. During the day, Rosa had white-washed the dark gray walls, scrubbed the floor, and washed the windows, through which before the light could scarcely penetrate. The bed had been supplied with clean, fresh straw; the blanket had been washed; and a pillow from her own bed had been placed upon this.

"O Rosa! Thou art indeed an angel of mercy to me. Truly, filial affection can smooth the rugged pathway of life for parents, and strew it with flowers. It can change a dreary cell into a pleasant room. But tell me, my child, how was it possible for you to accomplish all this in so short a time?"

Rosa replied: "There is an old soldier here, who was

a plasterer and mason, who occasionally does some work about the premises. A week ago he was sick, and my mistress, at my request, sent him a little broth. When time permitted, I sat down and conversed with him a little. One day, of course without knowing who I was, he began to speak of you with great affection and regard. He said, that in a certain battle, which had almost been lost through the rashness of Kunerick, and which was gained only through your coolness and intrepidity, he was dangerously wounded, and would have been left to perish on the field, if you had not taken compassion on him. Last evening, though with trembling and fear, I told him who I was, and begged him to assist me in rendering your prison a little more comfortable. I was apprehensive he would make objections, but he approved of my course, and cheerfully aided me,—nay, he performed the most of the labor himself. He said he did not care much whether Kunerick might be apprised of it or not."

Edelbert said, "I do not remember of having assisted that man, but this manifestation of his gratitude deeply affects my heart. You see, my child, how favors bestowed upon others, though forgotten by us, will never be without their reward."

Rosa now opened her basket, and placing the provisions she had brought, upon the table, said, "This evening, father, we will sup together, for we have not enjoyed that pleasure since the dreadful night on which we were so suddenly separated." The supper consisted of a bowl of milk, a dish of the choicest mushrooms fried in butter, some lettuce out of the garden, and good, fresh bread.

"But tell me, child," said Edelbert, as he looked upon the bed and then upon the table, "tell me, whence do you get all these things? For, much as I stand in need of them, I cannot enjoy them if they are not honestly obtained. Let not the affection of my daughter for her father, tempt her to commit one dishonest act."

Rosa smilingly replied, "Be not uneasy on that score, I can explain all satisfactorily. The milk, and bread, and butter, were for my own supper, the mushrooms Agnes brought me yesterday, and the lettuce is of my own planting in the garden, of which, as you perceived, there was a great abundance; the straw was given me by the hostler; the blanket is not, as you imagine, a new one, but the old one, washed, and the pillow is from my bed."

"I am satisfied," said he, "and it was wrong in me to entertain such unfounded suspicions of my daughter. No, Rosa, you will always remain honest and upright. I have supped with the emperor, but never, never with such a relish as I have supped this evening."

Never had Rosa's happiness equaled to that which she now experienced in alleviating the sorrows of her father. She realized the truth of the passage of Scripture, "It is more blessed to give than to receive." Oh! How happy might the rich be if they knew this! How happy might children be, who are able to render their aged and needy parents comfortable! Rosa now had to leave her father, and attend to her duties at home. She therefore bade her father good night. The pleasing reflection of being the parent of so excellent a daughter, so occupied Edelbert's mind, that he could not sleep until nearly midnight; and when he fell asleep, the idea flitted before his mind in the most delightful visions of his dreams.

Every day this dutiful daughter gave her father new proofs of her affection. She made many sacrifices of her own comfort, and endured privations that she might assist him. She ate but sparingly, that she might give him the food which was set apart for her. Her scanty wages, the gifts of money she received from strangers, and the fruit and other presents which Agnes occasionally brought, were all reserved for him; she lived entirely for him.

After the lapse of a few weeks, the steward, having been sent to look after matters at the castle, and to attend to some special business for the count, visited the prisoners. When he entered Edelbert's apartment, he was very much surprised, and shook his head. "Kunerick must not know this, or else a gloomier cell might await me. What a difference a little lime and soap, with a little labor, can make. This cell has been changed into a pleasant room, whilst, through neglect and idleness, many a dwelling, otherwise comfortable, becomes unfit to be occupied."

When they had left the room, he said to Rosa, "Girl! I will not censure you for your kindness to this unfortunate knight; it corresponds with your general good-nature. But mark me! Let not your sympathy so far mislead you, as to make an attempt to induce and aid him to escape. Escape would, indeed, be utterly impossible—the wall is too high, the gates too well secured and guarded, and the dyke too broad and deep to be crossed while the drawbridge is hoisted; yet even an attempt of this kind on his part might prove my ruin. I should lose my station, and my wife and children would have to suffer want. Yes, I am fearful that Kunerick, who is very passionate, might, in a fit of anger, pierce me through with his sword. My life is pledged for the security of the prisoners."

Rosa faithfully promised that she would not be so ungrateful as to requite his kindness by such an act of treachery.

"I am satisfied," said he; "I take your word for it; you have never deceived me; you are too honest and true to prove unfaithful to your master."

## Chapter Thirteen.

### ROSA IS COUNSELED AND
### DIRECTED BY HER FATHER.

HILST Edelbert enjoyed much comfort through the filial affection of his daughter, and Rosa found the greatest satisfaction in the happiness of her father, a great change took place in Kunerick's circumstances. His palace had long been the abode of prosperity and plenty. But sorrows and afflictions pay no regard to bolts, and bars, and drawbridges,—they find as easy an entrance there as elsewhere.

The accounts of the war in which Kunerick had engaged with a powerful knight, from motives of pride and ambition, were of the most alarming character. Kunerick himself was wounded, his army put to flight, his camp plundered, and he now lay suffering from his wounds in a distant castle. Instead of being able to send the spoils of victory to his family, they had to furnish him with money, and even with the necessaries of life. His wife did not venture to visit him, as she could not command a sufficient number of men to constitute a safe escort. His enemies, emboldened by success, became more insolent and daring. They had already interceded and taken some wagons with provisions, which had been purchased at a distance, and designed for the support of his family and his dependants at the castle. His wife and children had to content themselves with the most ordinary provisions, and even these almost failed. In addition to this, his children took the smallpox, and his wife, worn down by care and sorrow, also became dangerously ill.

Rosa had obtained the most minute information of their circumstances from her mistress. She never went to the castle, except when she was sent on an errand, nor had she ever entered the apartments of the lady and her children, though several occasions offered when she might have done so with propriety. Whenever she met the knight, or any of his family, she thought of the injustice done to her father, and gradually, before she was aware of it, a feeling of dislike, and almost of hatred, began to rankle in her bosom, not only against Kunerick, but also against his wife and children.

Rosa related what she had heard from her mistress concerning Kunerick and his family, with an almost imperceptible smile of satisfaction upon her countenance. "Now," said she, "they may learn by experience what sorrows and afflictions are; their pride may yet be humbled. This haughty woman, who has been clothed so richly, and fared so sumptuously, may yet be obliged to content herself with more ordinary apparel, and she and her children to subsist upon meaner fare; and the proud, over-bearing knight, who has caused us, and many others, so much distress, may experience the truth of the proverb: 'With whatsoever measure ye mete, it shall be measured to you again.'"

"Rosa, Rosa," said her father, "do I hear you speak thus? Must I see, on your usually mild countenance, a smile of satisfaction at another's woe? My child, this feeling is wrong, is sinful. O let not envy and malice poison your generous heart. It is true, the knight has treated me ill; he has hated me without a cause, and thrown me into prison. But you are not unacquainted with the example and precepts of the Saviour. Does not He say, 'Love your enemies; bless them that curse you; do good to them that hate you; and pray for them which despitefully use you, and persecute you?' And you would requite the evil which Kunerick has done to us, upon his wife and innocent children? Rosa, Rosa, let not your affection for your father cause you so far to forget the precepts of our holy religion, as to indulge a feeling of hatred towards our enemy. God knows, I do not hate Kunerick. If he were in danger, surrounded by his enemies, or a band of robbers, at the risk of my life I would hasten to his aid and rescue him. And could you, my child, if a change of fortune should take place; if you should be raised to affluence, and they should be brought to poverty and distress, could you turn a deaf ear to the entreaties of this lady and her children, and harden your heart, and close your hands and doors against them?"

"No," said Rosa, much affected by what her father had said; "I would, I could not. I would aid them to the extent of my ability."

"I doubt it," said her father; "if you cannot even meet them without indulging unfriendly feelings, how could you feel inclined to do good to, and assist them? Banish this evil feeling from your bosom; ever meet them in the most friendly manner; and especially, as they are in affliction, visit them, and, with the permission of your mistress, aid them as far as you can.

"Imagine not, that in giving this advice, I am actuated by worldly policy and self-interest,—thinking, through your kindness to them, to gain the favor of the enemy, in whose power I am, so that he may liberate me, and perhaps restore to us the possessions he has taken from us. By no means. If this were my motive, then the benevolence I profess would not deserve the name; it would be mere hypocrisy, of which I should have cause to be ashamed.

"No, true benevolence is a heavenly plant, and cannot grow in a heart full of selfishness. It can only flourish in an upright and holy heart. True benevolence is only the image, the reflection, of that heavenly love, which constitutes the spirit, the essence of our holy religion, and which will be found in every pious heart. God emphatically is love. He causes his sun to shine, and his rain to descend even upon the rebellious. He desires that even the vilest may turn from the evil of their ways, and live. For such, the Saviour shed his blood and died. His was pure, universal love—benevolence in the highest sense of the term. Like his, our benevolence must be pure and universal. We must love all, as brethren, and endeavor to do them good. Our greatest enemies are not to be excluded from this love. We should be ready to make sacrifices, in order that we may do good to others. We must love them as ourselves. Yes, our love must rise and wing its flight to heaven. God is worthy of our supreme affection, and we must not only love Him above all things, but also seek to imitate Him in the exercise of this love.

"Without this supreme love to God, and love to all men, even to our enemies, we shall never be fit for heaven. A soul destitute of love would be miserable even there. He who hates his fellow-man, is yet unprepared for it. Love is the fountain of all its blessedness; it is love which constitutes heaven.

"It is the great end of our being, to have this heavenly plant growing and flourishing in our hearts, that it may bring forth its appropriate fruit in our lives. The love of those objects that are of a low and groveling nature, will leave no room in the heart for this heavenly affection. It is on this account, that God sends sorrows and afflictions to divest us of pride, selfishness, and the inordinate love of the world, that our hearts may be prepared for this holy love. This may have been the design of God in depriving us of rank and station in life,—of our possessions and our enjoyments. There may yet be something in our hearts that is not right in the sight of our God, and he designs to show us how unworthy of our affections these objects are, and to induce us to seek such objects as are worthy of the love of beings possessed of immortal minds. Let us discern and acknowledge God's kind gracious designs toward us, and not frustrate them, by indulging a malevolent disposition towards our enemies, and thus rob ourselves of the blessings and benefits of affliction."

Rosa listened with marked attention, and replied: "You are right, father. Oh how far is my heart from being as it ought to be, and as I desire it to be. With the help of the Lord, I will endeavor to banish this evil feeling from my bosom. I will seek to love God above all things, and my fellow-men as myself. I will endeavor to love Kunerick, and his wife and children. And if sufferings and afflictions are designed for our good—designed to make us better—I will willingly suffer as long as our Father in heaven sees best to continue them; for it is written: 'All things shall work together for good to them that love God.'"

Rosa sought to profit by the instructions of her father. She no longer indulged unkind feelings towards any of Kunerick's family. His children, having again recovered, were sometimes taken out by their nurse, and one day came with her to the steward's house. Rosa treated them kindly, entered into conversation with them, and found them to be amiable and mild, and she wondered how she could ever have indulged any other feeling than affection for them. Agnes had brought her a pair of doves, and a young kid, as a gift. These she presented to the children; and in a short time she became much attached to them, and they, in turn, as much attached to her. She bitterly reproached herself for having indulged feelings of hostility towards these innocent children. "I have thus robbed myself of the delightful satisfaction of doing good, and thus my error was also my punishment. My father was right in saying, that it affords us inward satisfaction to cherish a forgiving and friendly spirit, whilst the indulgence of a contrary spirit makes us uneasy and unhappy." An opportunity, however, soon offered, to test more fully Rosa's obedience to the excellent instructions of her father.

## Chapter Fourteen.

### ROSA'S NOBLE DEED IN
### RESCUING EBERHARD.

HE children had now, for some days, been confined to the house, in consequence of the unpleasantness of the weather, and Rosa had not seen them for a week. The clouds had, however, disappeared, and the sun shone again, and animated all with new life. The busy husbandmen were in the fields, gathering in their crops. Thekla, who had charge of the children, had taken them out into the courtyard to enjoy the delightful morning.

In the centre of the yard, not far from the palace, there was a well, handsomely enclosed with a stone wall, and covered with a peaked roof, supported by six pillars, beautifully carved, in pure Gothic style. The well was very deep, and it required nearly ten minutes to raise a single bucket of water by means of a large wheel and windlass. This well was regarded as a curiosity at the castle, and no stranger ever left the place without visiting it. In order to give visitors an idea of its great depth, small stones were thrown into it, and all were surprised at the time that elapsed before they heard the sound occasioned by their striking the water below. A candle was also frequently let down into it, and as the light was reflected by the drops of water which hung upon the stones, the wall appeared studded with diamonds. It was said that before the roof was placed over it, persons who descended to clean the well could see the stars glittering in the sky at noon-day. The well was surrounded with a beautiful green-sward, and bushes which bore small red berries; to which the birds resorted, and where they sometimes built their nests.

On this grass-plat Kunerick's three children were playing. Itha and Emma were engaged in gathering the small berries from the bushes, and stringing them together to hang around their necks. These they called their coral necklaces. Eberhard amused himself with throwing stones into the well. While he was gathering some stones, a little bird flew into the bucket. Eberhard saw it, and said to his sisters, "Stay, I'll catch that little bird, and we will have some sport with it." He leaned over the wall to reach it, lost his balance, and fell into the well. His little sisters were very much frightened, and raised a loud cry of distress. Thekla, the nurse, who had left the children to take care of themselves, heard their cry, and hastened to the spot. But when they told her that Eberhard had fallen into the well, she was so much alarmed that she knew not what to do. Contrary to her expectations, she heard his cries, and on looking down into the well, saw him hanging by his clothes, which had been caught by a hook fixed in the wall! "What shall I do? What shall I do?" she cried as loud as she could. The mother of the children heard the cry, but was unable to leave her bed. The men were all in the fields, assisting to gather the harvest, and the affrighted girl knew not whither to run for help.

Rosa, hearing the cries of the girl, hastened to the

well. Instantly she determined, if possible, with the help of the Lord, to save the child. "Quick!" said she to Thekla, "Assist me to get into the bucket—now let it down slowly." As she descended deeper and deeper into the cold, damp well, and the light gradually became more and more dim, she shuddered and trembled, and the cold sweat stood in drops upon her forehead. "Stop! Stop!" cried she, as she reached the place where the boy was hanging. She then endeavored to loosen the boy's clothes and take him into the bucket, but she found it almost beyond her power, as she had to hold on to the chain with one hand. "Aid me, O thou gracious God!" she cried, and made another powerful effort, which was successful. The boy, fearful of falling, clung with both arms around her neck. "Hoist! Hoist!" cried she to the girl, and, nerved with hope, she turned the wheel, until Rosa and the child were raised above the top of the well. Thekla quickly fastened the wheel, it was a difficult matter for Thekla, yet trembling in every joint, to lift the boy out of the bucket. She caught hold of the chain with a hook which was made for that purpose, and attempted to draw it towards her, but whenever she let go the hook, the bucket swung over to the other side. It was a fearful sight for the mother, who, from the window of her chamber, witnessed several unsuccessful attempts. At last Rosa said to Thekla, "Give the bucket a gentle push, and swing it to and fro; then watch the opportunity, and when it swings over to your side, quickly lay hold of the boy." She did so, and succeeded. "Thank God, my child is saved!" cried the almost frantic mother.

Thekla now endeavored to assist Rosa, but she again told her to swing the bucket gently to and fro; and when it neared one of the pillars, Rosa caught hold of it, stepped upon the wall in safety, and leaped upon the green, on which the trembling child sat. The deed was one performed from the impulse of the moment, and without any time for reflection. When Rosa, therefore, thought of what she had done, the danger she had been in of perishing in the well, she could scarcely speak, and almost fainted. In a little while, however, she recovered, and after expressing her gratitude to God she hastened to tell her father of the circumstance. He could scarcely give credit to her story, and thought it almost impossible. When, however, he was assured that it was really so, he said, "You have gained a great victory. You have conquered yourself, and hazarded your life to do good to an enemy. This is a greater conquest than that achieved by the man who storms and takes the strongest fortress, for it is said, 'He that is slow to anger is better than the mighty, and he that ruleth his spirit than he that taketh a city.' But be not proud of your deed, it is God who enabled you to perform it; to Him alone belongs all the praise."

## Chapter Fifteen.

### ROSA MANIFESTS A NOBLE
### AND GENEROUS SPIRIT.

HEKLA had, in the mean time, taken the child to his mother, who, for the moment, felt nothing of her sickness, and ran to embrace him. She asked him again and again, whether he felt any pain. He was not materially injured, but was very pale and faint, from terror. "The Lord has spared him," she exclaimed; "I will endeavor to train him up in His fear. My child, what anguish have you occasioned me by your carelessness! How often have I cautioned you not to go to the well, nor to go near the horses, nor climb upon trees! Your disobedience has almost cost you your life. What would your father have said, if you had been killed by your fall! Oh! Henceforth seek to be more obedient."

"But where," said she, turning to Thekla, "where is the noble girl who saved my child? Was it not the poor collier's daughter? Go, Thekla, haste, and let her come here directly, that I may thank her. This noble action must not remain without its reward."

Thekla hastened, and found Rosa sitting at the bedside of the steward's children, who were sick. "Come," said she, "you must instantly go to the castle; the lady wishes to see you, and no doubt will reward you most generously."

Rosa's sensitive heart was wounded to hear even

an intimation given of a reward, and felt but little inclined to go. She however thought, if she refused to go, her motives might be misconstrued, and the lady be displeased. She therefore obeyed the summons. In the most unassuming manner, and with a blush of modesty on her countenance, she entered the lady's chamber. The little boy whom she had rescued was lying on a bed, and the mother sat beside him. As soon as she saw Rosa, she approached her, took her hand, and kissed her, saying, "My dear girl, I owe you a thousand thanks! What a noble act you have performed! From what indescribable sorrow and grief have you saved me! Had it not been for you, my dear boy, instead of sleeping so sweetly on his bed, would be lying cold and lifeless in yonder well! You have saved my child from the grave: from this moment you shall be treated as one of my children. I will be a mother to you, and you must from henceforth live with me."

"But," addressing herself to Thekla, she said, in a firm but mild tone, "I cannot longer keep you in my service. You have neglected your duty, and, instead of being a watchful guardian over my children, you have almost become the murderer of my darling boy. I will pay you your wages this evening, and to-morrow you must leave my house."

Thekla wept aloud and begged for forgiveness. She fell upon her knees, and entreated her mistress not to send her away. "I am a poor orphan," said she; "I know not where to go, or with whom to find a home! Oh! Do keep me; I will be more careful in the future."

"You have promised so often," replied the lady, "that I cannot rely upon your promises any longer. I am sorry, indeed, to be compelled to discharge you; but merely to oblige you, I cannot expose my children to continual danger, and myself to constant fear and apprehension. You must go, and I hope, when you obtain another place, you will be more careful and attentive to your duties."

"May I, dearest madam," said Rosa, "without incurring the charge of being bold and officious, speak a word in Thekla's behalf? The charge you bring against her is true. She has neglected the important trust committed to her. Her carelessness has given your parental feelings a shock, the effects of which will be felt for some time, and has almost cost the life of your child. This dreadful accident will prove an effectual warning to Thekla, and I am certain she will be more careful in the future.

"But, if Thekla has erred, did she not exert herself to the utmost in aiding me to save the boy? Did you not, from your window, see that she risked her own life, in her attempts to reach the boy and take him out of my arms? And now, will you remember only her fault, and not bear in mind the essential aid she rendered me, without which the child could not possibly have been saved?

"Has not God heard the prayers that you offered for your son, and in the same hour would you turn a deaf ear to the supplications of a penitent at your feet? God has shown mercy to you; act like him, and show mercy to Thekla. You have a favorable opportunity to manifest the sincerity of your gratitude to God, for His mercy in saving your child, by extending mercy to this distressed girl, and receiving her again into your

favor. Thekla and I rejoiced with you, when your child
was rescued; and will you, ere yet the tears of joy have
been wiped from your eyes, press the bitterest tears
from another's eyes, without being willing, with the
kindest hand, to wipe those tears away, and by freely
forgiving Thekla, cause no more to flow? No, no! I
know your generous heart better than this.

"Moreover, I can never consent to take Thekla's
place, which you have been so kind as to offer me. I
would consider it wrong, yea sinful, to contribute in
the remotest degree to dispossess a poor servant-girl
of her place of service, and thus build my happiness
upon the ruin of another."

The lady looked upon the supposed collier's
daughter with wonder and astonishment. "I know
not which to admire most," said she, "your heroic
act, or the noble sentiments of your heart. Who could
withstand so able an intercessor? Thekla is forgiven,
and shall retain her place. But you shall also live
with me; I cannot do without you. At present, I am
not able adequately to reward you for what you have
done, but when my husband returns, which I expect
will be very soon, your reward shall be proportioned
to the service you have rendered us. But, meanwhile
you shall leave the service of the steward's wife, and
become my daughter, my friend, my companion; for
you were never destined for a situation like that which
you now occupy."

Rosa's heart was touched by the conduct of the
lady, and she could not but be grateful for the generous offers which she made; and might probably have

accepted them, had it not been for the situation of her father. She knew that if she accepted them, she could not visit him as frequently, nor minister to his wants; and to disclose the secret, that she was Edelbert's daughter, she thought might be premature and dangerous; nor could she think of doing so without first asking his advice. She therefore replied, "Pardon me, madam, when I say that I must decline this generous offer also, and believe me when I assure you that I am not insensible to your kind intentions. For, on the one hand, it is better, when, through the assistance of God, we have done good to our fellow-men, not to receive praise and reward for them, for then our reward shall be great in heaven. On the other hand, I have learned to be satisfied with my present situation. It is not rank and station in life which truly enable us, but the manner in which we perform the duties, and endure the trials of the station in which God has placed us. In my present station I have frequent opportunities to perform many acts of kindness to the prisoners. I am happy now; render me not unhappy by your goodness."

"Mysterious girl," said the lady, "I cannot understand you. Your remarks concerning happiness in your present situation, and unhappiness if you should accept my offers, appear strange—passing strange, to me. Is there then no way in which I can serve you? Ask what you please, and I promise you, upon my honor, if it be in my power, it shall be granted."

"I take you at your word, madam," replied Rosa; "but give me a reasonable time to reflect upon what I shall ask. The time may not be far distant when you can render me an important service. Until then, permit me to remain in my happy obscurity. But—pardon me, I must now go, and wait upon the sick child of my mistress."

# Chapter Sixteen.

## ROSA'S RANK AND STATION IN
## LIFE IS DISCOVERED.

HE lady of the castle was held in high esteem, both on account of the generous feelings of her heart, and her intellectual attainments. She knew how to appreciate Rosa's nobleness of soul: she entertained for her the highest esteem, and desired to make her happy, but she could not unravel the air of mystery which hung around her. She believed, and not without sufficient ground, that she was more than an ordinary servant-girl.

"Sentiments such as she entertains," said she, "language so chaste and refined, as she uses—manners so modest and unassuming, are never met with in a poor collier's daughter. She entered my chamber in a manner so free and yet so modest, and conversed with as much ease and fluency as though she had received a finished education, and moved in the best circles in life. This surprises me most of all, and interests me in her behalf, more than the deed of noble daring she performed in saving my child. And what can be the reason that she declines my offer to receive her into my family, and prefers her present state of arduous servitude? There is something which I cannot understand. Can it be, that there is guilt in that bosom? Is there a secret connected with her history, which she would be ashamed to have others know? This I cannot bring myself to believe. No, in her bosom there can be no guilt. Yet henceforth, I will watch her closely."

She sent for the old bailiff, told him her suspicions, and charged him to watch all her movements. He did so, for some days, and always brought the most favorable intelligence concerning her. One morning, however, he came in great haste, and very much agitated, and reported that, at midnight, when all was quiet about the castle, Rosa visited their greatest enemy, the knight Edelbert, and remained for hours with him, in his prison. "This matter," said he, "appears very suspicious, and may be fraught with no small degree of danger to us. This girl, in the absence of the steward, has been intrusted with the keys of the prison, and has both talents sufficient to devise, and courage enough to carry into effect a plan of deliverance. Yet, though I heard them converse with each other, I could not make out what was the subject of their conversation."

The lady was not a little surprised at the intelligence, and remarked, "Edelbert is our worst enemy. This, my husband has frequently told me. When I interceded in his behalf, and intreated that his situation might be rendered more comfortable, my husband gave me such unfavorable accounts of him, that I could not doubt that he entertained the most hostile feelings towards us; and that this girl should be on such terms of intimacy with him, I do not at all relish. But I will go and convince myself."

She told the bailiff to go, and watch again, and when he saw Rosa go to the prison, immediately to bring her word, but not to breathe a word about the affair to any one on the premises.

A few nights after this, the old bailiff came and said, "Now, madam, is your time; Rosa has just gone to the prison." She immediately threw her mantle around herself, and hastened to the door of the cell. "It is indeed no honorable employment in which I am engaged," said she to herself. "To go secretly to the door of an apartment, and to spy out, and listen to the secrets of others, is a mean and despicable employment. But I do it only because I am concerned for the welfare of the girl herself, and also because I feel concerned for our own safety." The door was closed, but not latched, and a dim lamp was burning in the cell. She could distinctly hear every word of the following conversation.

EDELBERT.—These peaches are delicious; they are of the same kind we had in our garden in the castle. Peaches were always my favorite fruit. How beautiful the tinge, like the modest blush on the virtuous maiden's cheek; how fragrant the smell, how delicious the taste!

ROSA.—I can scarcely refrain from tears, when I look upon these peaches: they recall to my mind so many associations of pleasures past, perhaps never to be enjoyed again. Oh that I could again gather peaches from our tree in the garden, and present them to you in a basket, decorated with flowers, as I once did!

EDELBERT.—Be thankful that you were able to bring me these. If I understand you correctly, this tree had scarcely a dozen of peaches this season, and out of this number, the lady gave you three; she is very kind to you indeed.

ROSA.—And because she is so, I often feel as though

I must tell her that I am your daughter; she would not divulge the secret, and would be the most proper person to be intrusted with it, as she might embrace the first favorable opportunity to intercede with her husband for your release from prison.

EDELBERT.—I am of a different opinion. You cannot imagine how Kunerick hates me. The heart of this good lady may be as soft and tender as these peaches, but his is as hard as the peach stone.

ROSA.—I think, however, if Kunerick is informed that your daughter, with the help of God, saved the life of his child, he would not let you die in prison. And if I were to throw myself upon my knees before him, and, with tears, entreat him, he would certainly liberate you.

EDELBERT.—Do not deceive yourself, my daughter; I know him too well. He may commend your noble and praiseworthy act; he may even offer to reward you liberally; but his enmity is too deep-rooted to permit him ever to listen to any appeals, however strong. You might as well attempt to bend the tallest oak of the forest, as to move him.

ROSA.—But, dearest father, if we could convince him, that though he has robbed you of all your possessions, and treated you so cruelly, you bear him no ill-will; that you would aid him to the extent of your power; that you taught me to love him and his family, and to do them good; that without your instructions I would probably not have run to the well upon the first cry of the children, nor risked my life to save his boy; and that therefore they owe the life of the child chiefly to you—would not this move and melt his obdurate heart? Or, think you, that nothing can have any effect upon him? That it is altogether impossible to change his feelings towards you?

EDELBERT.—Possible it may be, but it is not at all probable. For the present, however, nothing can be done; until he comes I must remain in prison. Even if his wife should be disposed to set me at liberty, without his permission I could not accept of it. He might treat her ill for her kindness to me. Even if she would permit me to leave my cell and walk about in the courtyard, the passionate and ill-disposed man might entertain a thousand unfounded suspicions. For the present, therefore, Rosa, you must divulge nothing, and I must remain in prison, until God, in his wise providence, opens a way of escape. I would not, by any means, bring the good lady into trouble. The Lord, in due time, will help us. But, Rosa, I perceive your heart is full and sad—enough of this for the present....

The lady had heard enough to satisfy her mind; she hastened to her chamber, not to sleep, but to reflect upon what she had heard. "This supposed collier's daughter," said she, "is indeed a young lady of rank and fortune! In order to be near, and assist her father, she has clothed herself in the humblest garb, and entered upon a hard service. The fruit and presents received from me, she never tasted, but preserved them for her father. Out of affection for him, she declined every offer I could make to render her situation more comfortable; and chose rather to endure toil and fatigue, than lose the pleasure of visiting him in his afflictions. What a noble soul she must possess! How happy must be the parents of such a child! And this girl, the daughter of a man whom we have confined in prison and loaded with chains, saved my child—and this father inspired her heart with such feelings and sentiments, and taught her to perform actions so noble! He cannot be a bad man; a man like him need not be feared. He shall be free! He shall be reinstated in his own castle. If it were in my power, he should be released from his prison this very night, and with to-morrow's dawn should be on his way to Linden castle. But this is impossible; the old bailiff here, would never consent to such a proposition; nor could our castellan at Linden be prevailed upon to admit him there. If I attempted such a thing, my husband would never forgive me; when he returns, however, I will use my utmost endeavors to persuade him to do justice to the good knight, and his excellent daughter, and if arguments fail, I will try the efficacy of tears and entreaties, which, with a husband who really loves his wife, are almost irresistible."

"But how, in the mean time," thought she, "shall I conduct myself towards Rosa? Shall I tell her that I know that she is Eldelbert's daughter, and treat her as a young lady, in a manner becoming her rank in life? What a sensation would not this create among all our people at the castle! The sturdy old bailiff would never permit Rosa to see her father again, and would place a constant guard around the prison. It would only render the situation of daughter and father more miserable. For the present, therefore, I will keep the secret in my own bosom; and content myself with aiding them, as far as I can, without creating suspicion—leaving the development of the secret to a more propitious moment."

## Chapter Seventeen

ROSA INTERCEDES ON BEHALF OF HER FATHER.

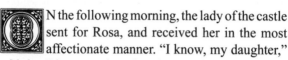 N the following morning, the lady of the castle
sent for Rosa, and received her in the most
affectionate manner. "I know, my daughter,"
said she, "that you take a deep interest in, and sincerely
sympathize with the knight who is imprisoned in our
fortress. I admire the goodness of your heart, and as
you are placed in circumstances that enable you to
afford him but little aid, I will henceforth supply you
with the means necessary for his comfort." The good
lady secretly supplied Rosa with substantial food, and
conducted herself towards her in such a manner as
entirely to lull the rising suspicions of the old bailiff.
She daily went to the steward's house, in company
with her children, under the pretense of seeing the
preserver of her child, and, by her personal attention
to Rosa, influenced the steward's wife to treat her
more mildly, and greatly to diminish her labors.

Rosa was often sent for, to come to the castle, and
was permitted to bring the children with her. The poor
woman thought this a great privilege and honor for
her children, and prided herself upon having a servant
who stood so high in the estimation of the lady of the
castle. On this account she began to treat Rosa more
like a sister than a servant.

Meanwhile, the lady, with painful anxiety, looked
for the return of her husband. Had he not sent word

that he had recovered from his wounds, and would shortly return, she would have ventured to pay him a visit. After a few weeks, however, Kunerick, in company with the two knights, and the greater part of the soldiers who had been in the service, returned. The knights, officers, and soldiers, had decorated themselves with green oak leaves, and in true martial order entered the wide gates, amidst the loud blasts of the war bugle and the still louder shoutings of the warriors themselves. Kunerick leaped from his horse, embraced Hildegard his wife, and his children, who had come into the courtyard to welcome him to his home, and then proceeded with the knights and officers to the spacious main hall of the castle. After the first demonstrations of joy had subsided, and Kunerick had taken his boy upon his knee, his wife gave him a vivid and circumstantial account of the danger, and the wonderful and providential rescue of his child. Kunerick grew pale, and trembled as she related the facts. "So," said he, "you had wellnigh been drowned, and your father almost deprived the pleasure of seeing you again. What an affliction this would have been for your mother and myself. I shudder when I think of it. My son, you must be more careful in the future."

The mother brought the coat which the boy had on when he fell into the well, and showed the rent which the hook had made, and by which he hung suspended. Kunerick examined it carefully, and remarked, "It was well indeed that he was rescued so soon; a little longer delay,—a few moments more, and the few remaining threads would have broken, and he must have perished. The poor servant-girl has placed us under great obligations to her. It was a noble act—an act which deserves the highest encomiums. The prompt decision and the unexampled courage of the girl, greatly interest me in her favor. But have you rewarded her in a manner worthy so noble an action?"

"This I have left for you to do, my husband. All the reward I could have given appeared to me entirely too inadequate; yes, as nothing, compared with the deed she performed, and the service she rendered us. She risked her life in the attempt. I cannot express to you my feelings, when I saw her entering the bucket, and especially, when I saw her again hanging over the mouth of the deep well! Such a deed cannot be repaid with gold. I told her that when you returned, you would reward her—and I hope you will fully realize my expectations, and redeem my pledge."

Kunerick was almost overcome, as well by the generous sentiments of his wife, as the conduct of Rosa, and replied with much emotion, "I must see the girl instantly—send for her, send for her."

Rosa was sent for, and appeared before the knight in a modest and respectful manner, and yet with an air of dignity. The knight could not but feel a degree of respect for her, and exclaimed, "Welcome, thrice welcome, noble girl, preserver of my child! But let me think a little; I believe I have seen you before! Yes, yes, I remember I once met you at the steward's house; but then, I never would have thought that you were possessed of so heroic and noble a spirit. Well! well! I am under the greatest obligations for you; had it not been for you I should this day be the most miserable of fathers. Ask of me what you please—it shall be given you. Yes, I swear to you upon the honor of knighthood, that if you were to ask either of my castles—Forest or Linden castle—it should be yours."

Rosa, without much emotion, and with becoming propriety, replied: "My lord, you have made a great and solemn promise. The noble knights have been witnesses to it. I might ask a great favor, and you could not, with honor, deny my request. I, however, will ask no favor at your hands—I only plead for justice. Restore to me my father; and to my father the possessions you have taken from him."

"How? What did she say?" asked Kunerick, with surprise—"I robbed and plundered you? Who are you? And who is your father?"

"I am Rosa of Linden castle," replied she; "Edelbert is my father. Release him from prison, and restore to him his possessions."

The two knights, the officers, and all who were in the hall, were amazed, and looked upon each other with perfect astonishment. But Kunerick stepped back a few paces, put his hand to his forehead, and for a few moments stood unmoved like a statue. His long and deep-rooted enmity towards Edelbert appeared to rise in his bosom with increased violence. He became pale as death, looked wildly around, and muttered some unintelligible words. "One of my castles would I freely give," said he, "if any one else than the daughter of this man had saved my child."

All who were present were alarmed at the sudden change which came over the knight, and looked at each other, but were afraid to utter a word.

His wife, at length, ventured to speak to him: "I

have, only a few days since, found out that this supposed collier's daughter is Edelbert's child. Out of
love to her father, in order that she might visit him
in prison, and comfort him in his afflictions, she as-
sumed her present character—engaged herself as a
servant with the steward's wife—endured the severest
trials—suffered the greatest hardships—shared her
scanty wages, and even her food with him. I have felt
deeply pained to see her perform the toil and drudgery
of the lowest servant. I have not even intimated to her
that I knew she was Edelbert's daughter. I could not
do any thing in this matter, without your knowledge
and consent; but waited patiently for your return. But
now, dearest husband, let humanity and mercy prevail.
Even if Rosa had not rescued your son, her sincere
and devoted affection for her father should prevail
with you to be willing to be reconciled to a man who
is capable of training up a child like Rosa."

"By the honor of a knight," cried Siegbert, one of
the knights who was present, "the devoted affection
of Rosa to her father raises her higher in my estimation than the rescue of the boy. That act was the result
of the sudden impulse of the moment, and might
have been performed by a less noble spirit. But the
protracted sufferings, trials, and privations, which she
cheerfully endured for her father, are sure proofs of a
magnanimous mind. In such a heart there can be no
guile. Were I in your situation, I should not hesitate
long, as to the course I would pursue."

"Kunerick," said Theobald, the other knight, "If
Edelbert were, as you suppose, your sworn enemy, he
might have signally revenged himself. While you and

your soldiers were far from home, he, your supposed
enemy, was in your fortress, and his daughter was in
the possession of the keys of his cell. Almost any one
else would have embraced such an opportunity—fired
your castle at midnight, and, amidst the confusion
and tumult, made their escape. Kunerick, Kunerick,
you are laboring under a mistake; this man is not your
enemy, you need not fear to release him."

Kunerick stood looking upon the floor with a fixed
gaze, but said not a word. All beheld him in fearful
and anxious suspense. Rosa imploringly raised her
eyes to heaven; and the silence of death reigned in the
apartment.

After a short time, his wife approached him, and,
with tears in her eyes, said: "Dearest Kunerick, hear
me, I have but one remark more to make. You believe
that Edelbert is your implacable enemy, but you are
certainly mistaken. If it were so, how could I, your
wife, ask for his release? Would I not rather advise
you to keep him in confinement and to guard him
more closely? But that he is not our enemy, I will now
fully convince you.

"It was I, and I alone, who discovered that Rosa was
Edelbert's daughter. Until the moment she herself told
you, not a soul about the premises was aware of it,
but myself. The persons to whose care you intrusted
the castle, as little dreamed of it as yourself. Had it
not been for me, no one, not even your faithful old
bailiff, would ever have imagined that Rosa visited
the prison. Even at the hour of midnight I went unat-
tended through the long, dreary passage to Edelbert's
cell, and listened to their conversation. I could not

have ventured to do this, had I not been fearful that they were plotting some mischief. But what did I hear? Plottings of revenge! Of murder! No, no! Instead of this, nothing but the best wishes and prayers for our welfare. Edelbert said that 'If you were in danger and surrounded with enemies, he would risk his life to aid you. That even if the doors of your prison were opened, or should I propose to release him, he would not, without your knowledge and consent accept of his liberty. It was he, who instructed his daughter to love us, and to embrace every opportunity to do us good. Without his excellent instructions Rosa probably would not have rescued your child. How then could he be your enemy? And how can you longer hesitate to give him his liberty? O Kunerick, Kunerick! Why this delay. Rosa must not, shall not, leave this hall, without the promise of her father's immediate release. Humanity demands it, justice demands it, your solemn oath demands it."

Kunerick replied, in a low, muttering tone, "Rosa may take Linden castle, with all that belongs to it, I have no objections; but Edelbert shall stay where he is."

The little boy, seeing his mother and Rosa weep, and even the knights much affected, ran to his father and said, "Father, Rosa saved me out of the well, or else you never would have seen me again. When you were in the war, and we heard you were wounded, mother cried, and we all cried, and Rosa cried. Rosa loves us, and when you came home she was as glad as I was. But Rosa now cries for her father, who is in prison; she wants you to let him out. Won't you, father? Yes;

I know you will, and I will go with Rosa and tell her father he may come up here, and be free."

"Stop, stop, my boy: it is enough. I can hold out no longer. Your father, Rosa, is pardoned, and shall again be reinstated at Linden castle with all that formerly belonged to it. A man who has inspired his daughter with such feelings and sentiments cannot be a bad man."

"The Lord's name be praised," exclaimed his wife, and embraced her husband. Eberhard took, and kissed his father's hand. Rosa could not speak for joy.

"This is generous," said Theobald. "This act has rendered you doubly dear to me, and raised you high in my estimation."

"He has acted the part of a knight, in a manner becoming our rank. To be just, is better than to be brave, and to conquer ourselves is more praiseworthy than to subdue our enemies."

All the rest joined in praise of Kunerick. Bravo—noble—generous—just—right, cried one, and another, and another. And at last, they all, as if with one voice, exclaimed,

"Long live Kunerick, Hildegard, and Eberhard."

"Long live Edelbert and Rosa."

# Chapter Eighteen.

## ROSA BRINGS HER FATHER THE
## JOYFUL INTELLIGENCE OF HIS PARDON.

UNERICK, having conquered the unhallowed feelings of anger and revenge which had long held possession of his heart, felt like another man. The consciousness of having conquered himself and given heed to the dictates of humanity and of reason, imparted a satisfaction to which he had hitherto been an entire stranger. A calmness came over his spirit, like that which succeeds the tempest. The change in his countenance was noticed even by little Eberhard, who remarked, "How pleasant you look, father; just like mother and Rosa! Oh how I love you now!"

Rosa now, also, approached and expressed her gratitude, in the most glowing terms. "Come, come, Rosa," said he, "make not so much ado about the matter. I deserve no praise for having done what I ought to have done long ago. Let the matter rest, and come with me; we will go to your father, for I would consider it sinful to permit him longer to remain in prison. To you he is indebted for his pardon; and you shall be the bearer of the glad tidings to him. But Rosa, you must intercede for me, that he may forgive me the injustice I have done him."

Kunerick's wife now beckoned to her husband to come to the window, and spoke a few words to him

secretly. He nodded a cheerful assent. And Hildegard said to Rosa, "Come with me a few moments." She then led Rosa into an adjoining apartment, and placed before her apparel suited to the rank and station in life which she was again about to resume.

Rosa chose a neat, plain, white dress, and put it on; and put up her hair tastefully, in the same manner as she was accustomed to do, when at home, with her father. Hildegard was struck with her beauty, and her lady-like appearance; but thought it imprudent to pass any encomiums upon her, fearful lest it might awaken some latent feeling of pride or vanity.

"Here," said she, (handing Rosa a beautiful ebony box, elegantly inlaid with gold,) "this box contains the elegant and costly necklace and jewelry which belonged to your mother. My husband presented it to me when he returned from the taking of your castle. I have never worn it; I would have considered it a disgrace to adorn myself with ornaments obtained in a dishonorable manner. I have held it sacred as your property, and have long looked for the time when I could restore it to you. Receive it from my hands. Not a single diamond or pearl is wanting."

Rosa took the necklace with feelings of gratitude, but did not manifest that extreme delight, which Hildegard expected from one so young as Rosa. "O my sainted mother!" said Rosa, with tears in her eyes, "How vividly do these jewels recall to my mind those happy days when they decorated your person, while you were yet with us. These trinkets are only valuable to me as hallowed mementos of the best of mothers."

"This ring, set with diamonds," said she, as she took it from the box, "was my mother's wedding-ring; these bracelets, studded with pearls, were a present from the duchess. It appears to me as though I could see my mother standing before me, wearing these things as she used to do. Oh how frail and perishable are the children of men! These pearls yet remain, and these diamonds have lost none of their lustre, whilst the much loved form of my dear mother has returned to the earth, from which it was taken! What would man, the noblest work of God in this world, be, if he possessed not a spirit which will outlive his frail body, and which may be resplendent with glory, when these pearls and these diamonds shall have lost their lustre?"

"Dearest Rosa," rejoined Hildegard, "those tears, which glitter in your eyes, are more precious than all these pearls, and the sentiments and feelings of your heart are of greater value than these glittering diamonds. Yes, when your now blooming and youthful form shall have returned to dust, and when the all-destroying power of time shall have reduced to dust these precious stones, the noble and godly sentiments of your heart shall decorate your spirit more richly and beautifully than these gaudy trinkets can possibly ornament your perishing body. But we must now go and visit your dear father."

The lady accompanied Rosa to the prison. And Rosa, as she opened the door, exclaimed, "Thank God, dearest father, you are pardoned—you are free." But how great was her astonishment, as she entered the cell! There her father stood, clothed in the garb and style of a knight, with the golden chain and medal around his neck, and the two knights, Siegbert and Theobald, standing by his side. It was like a dream to her; she could scarcely realize it. "Is this reality," exclaimed she, "or is it the delusion of a dream, or the sportive fancy of a mind operated upon by a rapid succession of strange and almost unaccountable events?"

Hildegard, fearing that the change had been almost too great and sudden, and that it might be too much for Rosa's mind—already highly excited, explained to her the mystery of the change in her father's appearance. "You know," said she, "when I beckoned to my husband to come to the window in the main hall, we had some private conversation. It was then arranged that I should provide suitable apparel for you, and that he should do the same for your father. Moreover, it was thought advisable to prepare your father for the good tidings which you were to bring; lest the too sudden, and hasty announcement might have an injurious effect. This business was intrusted to the noble knights who stand at your father's side."

Edelbert and his daughter fondly embraced each other; and then, as he wiped the tears from his eyes, he remarked, "Tears are considered by the great of the world as a mark of a weak, effeminate, and ignoble mind, but I view them in many cases as a proof of a warm, generous, noble, godly heart. I am not ashamed of these tears, nor need I be, as long as I know that He whose heart beat with emotions, more warm, more generous, more noble, and more godly, than those which the heart of man ever felt, wept as he sympathized with the two mourning sisters, and when he thought of the dreadful destruction which the guilty inhabitants of Jerusalem were bringing upon themselves."

"Rosa," continued he, "with the help of God, you have gained a victory which a legion of well-armed and disciplined soldiers could not have achieved. These might have stormed this castle, and made Kunerick a prisoner; but the constraining influence of your love and affection for your father and for others, has conquered his heart, and changed an enemy into

a friend. But not to you belongs the glory. It is God
who has blessed you with this affection, and who has
crowned your efforts with success."

Edelbert, whose mind was so much occupied by
what had transpired, now, for the first time, noticed
the ornaments with which Rosa was decorated.
"Behold," he remarked, "God has not only granted
you that for which you prayed, and restored to your
father his liberty, but he has also returned the trinkets
and jewelry of your honorable mother, for which you
never asked Him.

"I have often, with painful feelings, thought of
the fact which you told me, that you had sold your
rings,—in order that you might procure the necessaries
of life for your father; but for these also, our heavenly
Father, contrary to your expectation, has made you a
rich compensation. Good done to others, and virtuous
actions performed, though forgotten by us, will never
be forgotten by Him, nor ever lose their reward."

The two knights, Siegbert and Theobald, were not a
little struck with the beauty and the lady-like appearance of Rosa. "Truly, my young lady," said Siegbert,
"you have made no small sacrifice in concealing
the tinge of the rose upon your cheeks with the vile
preparation made by Burkhard, and in disfiguring
your elegant form by the mean, and ill-suited garb of
a servant."

Rosa, considering this a mere compliment, deeply
blushed. But Theobald, observing that Rosa was
somewhat embarrassed by the remarks which the
other knight had made, quickly replied, "Beauty is
not this young lady's chief accomplishment; her filial

affection is of far greater importance, and renders her far more lovely. As an angel of mercy, she descended into her father's prison to minister to his wants; as an angel of mercy, she now appears to proclaim the liberty she has procured for him."

Rosa now thought of the promise she made, to ask her father to pardon the injuries Kunerick had done him. Edelbert replied, "You know that I have long since forgiven, and that I cherish no unfriendly feelings towards him." At this moment Kunerick, accompanied by his son, Eberhard, entered the cell. They exchanged salutations, promised to bury the past in oblivion, and pledged themselves to live in peace, harmony, and friendship with each other.

Edelbert felt much pleased to see the lad whose life Rosa had so miraculously preserved. Almost exhausted by what had just transpired, he seated himself upon the stone seat of the prison, took the boy upon his knee, and said, "God grant that you may prove a comfort to your parents, and become a good and pious man." "And," added Hildegard, "that his affection for his parents may be as sincere and devoted as that which your daughter cherishes for you; and that he may entertain the sentiments, and cherish the feelings, which she has always manifested."

The day closed with a sumptuous entertainment in the main hall of the palace. Edelbert and Rosa sat at the head of the table—Kunerick next to Edelbert, and Hildegard next to Rosa. All the guests were happy. Kunerick himself declared, "I have never felt as I do now. My implacable hatred towards Edelbert imbittered all my pleasures. I am convinced that anger and hatred proceed from, and are the offspring of hell, but love and friendship are plants of heavenly growth."

"Beware of the wine, gentlemen," said Edelbert: "wine has easily subdued those whom the enemy could not conquer, and has slain its thousands, where the sword has slain but its hundreds."

Kunerick smiled, and replied, "I recollect that you were always cautioning us against indulging in wine, when we were both but young men. It is right, and it would have been better for me had I imitated your example, and abstained altogether. The caution you give is proper, and I trust it will be duly regarded on this occasion."

At the close of the entertainment, which gave the greatest satisfaction to all the guests, the following sentiments were proposed:—

Edelbert rose and offered the following—"All honorable knights should live in peace and harmony, and never contend about trifles."

Theobald gave—"May all ladies imbibe the sentiments, cherish the feelings, and practise the virtues of Hildegard, Rosa, and Matilda."

Seigbert gave—"May all parents, in training up their children, imitate the example of Edelbert and Matilda; and may all children love and honor their parents as Rosa does her father."

Kunerick closed with—"May all parents experience as much happiness and comfort from the filial affection and virtuous conduct of their children, as Edelbert does from Rosa."

## Chapter Nineteen.

ROSA AND HER FATHER TAKE POSSESSION
OF THEIR CASTLE.

ARLY on the following morning, Kunerick came into Edelbert's chamber, roused him out of his sleep, and said, "Edelbert, I have called my men early, to get ready to accompany us to Linden castle this day; but Hildegard objects, because she thinks the castle, having now for some time been occupied by persons in our employment, needs some repairs. I doubt not but that she is correct; yet I would not have thought of it. You and Rosa will therefore be so good as to tarry with us for some time. You have spent many sorrowful days within these walls, and it is but just and right that you should also enjoy some days of happiness and pleasure."

Edelbert cordially assented to the proposed arrangement. Kunerick conducted him to the hall, where Siegbert and Theobald, with their attendants, were already waiting for them. After breakfast, Siegbert and Theobald bade them an affectionate farewell, and departed to their homes.

Kunerick, knowing that Edelbert would naturally feel anxious to return to his own castle, endeavored to engage his mind, and make the time pass as agreeably as possible. Hence he conducted him through his castle, showed him the gallery of the portraits of his ancestors; the armory, well stored with the implements of war, and with the spoils of his victories; the large, vaulted cellar, stocked with the choicest of wines; his large stables, conveniently arranged, and filled with well-trained and fiery war-steeds.

Hildegard, also, endeavored to render Rosa's stay as pleasant as possible, and, by engaging her attention continually, sought to divert her mind from her once happy home, to which she was now so very anxious to return. She took Rosa through her part of the house, and she showed her the excellent arrangements—the neatness, cleanliness, and order, which everywhere prevailed, Rosa was not only much gratified, but resolved to copy after so excellent an example.

Rosa having expressed a desire to visit her old mistress, the steward's wife, Hildegard immediately offered to accompany her. The steward was sitting at his door as they approached. As soon as he perceived them, he rose, descended the steps, and invited them into the house. He was much embarrassed at seeing Rosa, whom he had been so long accustomed to treat as a hired servant, now dressed in a manner becoming her station as the mistress of Linden castle.

"Rosa," said he—"pardon me, Miss Rosa I wished to say—who would ever have thought of this? I could rather have imagined that—that—yes, any thing, every thing else, than that my servant-girl was a lady of noble birth. It appears even now like a dream to me; I cannot realize it; and yet it appeared strange to me that a servant should take so deep an interest in a prisoner, to whom I thought she was a perfect stranger. But this explains the whole matter. My wife has been almost out of her senses ever since she heard it. She is continually talking of the manner in which she treated you—of the tasks she imposed upon you, and of the harsh and improper language she used towards you. But—but—"

"Where is she?" inquired Rosa, interrupting him; "call her, I must see her."

The children of the steward knew not what to make of all this; they stood in a corner, afraid to say a word. "Come here, Bertha, come here, Othmar," said Rosa; "don't you know me? I am Rosa, who used to be your nurse." The children, encouraged by her friendly manner, and her well-known voice, approached, and by degrees became quite familiar with her. "Oh! I wish you were our Rosa yet, and not a great lady as you now are," remarked little Bertha, with tears in her eyes, "for then you would stay with us; but now you are always at the castle, and are soon going away from us."

By this time the steward's wife, still more embarrassed than her husband, came in, pale and trembling. She attempted to speak, and to stammer out some excuses. Rosa, however, to relieve the poor woman from her confusion and embarrassment, said,

"My dear woman, there is no necessity for making excuses, and asking pardons now. In the situation of a servant, which I occupied while with you, I had no right to expect any other treatment than is due to a servant. I can give a flattering testimony in your favor, as a good, industrious, and cleanly housekeeper—a faithful and affectionate wife, and an indulgent and attentive mother, and a kind-hearted mistress, as long as nothing occurs to ruffle your temper, and rouse

your passion. If you could but overcome this, and
learn to govern yourself, no one would have any just
cause to complain of you. I know that this is a difficult
task–that it will not be the work of a single day, and
that it cannot be accomplished in your own strength.
But, by looking to the Lord for assistance, and by
perseverance, it can be accomplished. And when you
obtain another servant, who is willing and obedient,
do not expect that she will immediately be able to
attend to all the duties devolving upon her, as well
as you can. Give yourself some trouble to teach her
your mode of housekeeping; bear with her imperfec-
tions; point out her errors with mildness; instruct her
patiently, and you will feel happier in your own mind.
Avoid much wrangling and quarreling in your house,
and no one will ever have cause to complain of you."

The preparations for their reception having now
been completed, Kunerick and his wife, Edelbert and
Rosa, accompanied by a numerous retinue, proceeded
to Linden castle.

As they passed through Kunerick's domains, many
of the people out of every village and hamlet lined
the road, eager to see the two knights, Kunerick and
Edelbert, who, though formerly at variance with each
other, were now riding side by side, as the best of
friends. But more especially were they anxious to see
the young lady, who had sacrificed every thing to aid
her father, and who risked her life to save Kunerick's
child.

As soon, however, as they came within the bounds
of Edelbert's domains, all was quiet; no one was to
be seen, but a few small children. Edelbert could

not imagine what could be the reason of it, and was indulging in a variety of conjectures; but as he entered the gates of the courtyard, the mystery was solved; the whole court was filled with people. All his subjects were assembled, and arranged in appropriate order. On one side stood the boys, young men, and fathers: on the other, the girls, young women, and mothers of families. All were dressed in their best apparel. In behalf of the men, Burkhard was to address Edelbert and his company; in behalf of the females, Gertrude was to pay their respects to the ladies who accompanied Edelbert and Rosa.

Burkhard had applied to the old bailiff to write a speech for him in customary style, and committed it to memory. As the procession stopped before the steps of the castle, Burkhard, standing on a platform, erected for the occasion, in a most serious manner began:

"My Lords,—Since I have been appointed to address you on this interesting oc-oc-ca-sion, and to-to-pre-sent:—pardon me, dearest sir," continued he, "the moment I saw you, I forgot every word of the learned speech I had committed to memory. I can say no more, than that, having seen you reinstated in your possessions, I can now die in peace."

Now came Gertrude's turn; but she could not utter a word; her only language was tears of joy; but they were powerfully eloquent. The whole assembly, old and young, was excited, and all became orators.

"Long live Edelbert and Rosa! Long live Edelbert and Rosa!"

"Long live Kunerick and Hildegard!" rose the shout of the people, which was echoed and re-echoed from every side.

Edelbert and Rosa, with their company, now ascended the steps, and were welcomed by Siegbert and Theobald with their wives and children. At the door stood Agnes, the collier's daughter, clothed in white and decorated with flowers; she held in her hands a purple cushion trimmed with golden lace and tassels, on which were placed the keys to the castle. "Dearest lady," said Agnes, addressing Rosa; "you have not only rescued your father from prison, but have also put him again in possession of his estate; be pleased to accept of these keys, and present them to your father." Her father took the keys, and for some moments was silent, absorbed apparently in deep study. His thoughts reverted to that dreary night when his castle was stormed by Kunerick—when he was bound in chains, thrown upon a rough cart, and conveyed towards his enemy's castle. He almost fancied he heard again the lamentations and cries of Rosa, when he was so cruelly separated from her. With the sorrows of that night he contrasted his present joyful reception, which had been so happily arranged by Kunerick's wife. He could no longer contain himself, but taking off his hat, he turned to the assembled people, and exclaimed: "How wonderful are the ways of providence!—how unsearchable his plans! To Thee, O thou kind and gracious God, before all this people, would I give my most hearty thanks for all thy goodness bestowed upon me, thy unworthy servant!"

Preparations having been made, all were now invited to dinner. Edelbert, and those who came in the procession with him, together with some invited guests, repaired to the hall, and sat down to a sumptuous repast; while the people who had assembled, sat down at tables arranged in the court-yard, which were also bountifully furnished. Edelbert could not wait until dinner was over, but while his guests were yet seated at table, he quietly slipped out of the hall into the courtyard, and was welcomed among his subjects as a parent. Seeing Burkhard at the head of the table, he hastened to him, extended his hand, and said, "Thou old, faithful servant, how shall I reward you and your wife for the kindness bestowed upon my daughter, when, houseless and forlorn, she fled to you for refuge? You and yours shall never leave my castle. You are not too old to attend to the office of steward, which will not prove so laborious as the life of a collier who is exposed to every kind of weather. Your good wife, who supplied Rosa, and in part myself also, with clothing of your own manufacture, shall superintend my domestic affairs; and Agnes, who acted the part of a sister to Rosa in her distress, shall now be her constant companion in the days of her prosperity."

Edelbert now passed around the tables—spoke most affectionately to all the guests—assured them of his undiminished regard for them, and expressed the hope that their feelings towards him had undergone no change. They assured him that they were willing to devote their all, even their lives, to promote his happiness. Kunerick, who had missed Edelbert, followed him, and heard the assurances of mutual regard from him and his people, remarked: "Truly, virtue and goodness are stronger than might. It is far better to be loved, than to be feared." Edelbert replied: "A ruler and master whom the wicked fear, and whom the good esteem and love, is by far the happiest and best."

# Chapter Twenty.

### THE CONCLUSION.

EDELBERT and Kunerick, Rosa and Hildegard, visited each other frequently. In every undertaking of importance, Kunerick called upon Edelbert for advice. And Rosa looked upon Hildegard as upon a parent, and sought to profit by her instructions. The friendship and harmony which now existed, and the mutual exercise of kindness and affection, were not only a source of the greatest pleasure to them, but also one of the best methods of cultivating and strengthening these feelings, and thus rendering them happier and better.

For some time Kunerick did not visit Linden castle, and, by his apparently cold and formal behaviour, even discouraged Edelbert and Rosa from visiting him. One morning, however, unexpectedly and in great haste, he appeared before Linden castle, upon his fiery steed, covered with foam, and invited them to accompany him immediately to his castle. They at once perceived that he had some project in view, but could form no conjecture of what it might be: nor could they, in any wise, elicit the secret from him. They, however, were soon ready to accompany him. When they arrived at his castle, he would scarcely give them time to pay their respects to his lady. "Edelbert," said he, "you must instantly accompany me, and Rosa and Hildegard shall follow us!" He now took Edelbert's arm, and conducted him through the long, dark passage which led to the cell in which Edelbert had been imprisoned.

"What means all this?" said Edelbert. Rosa trembled, whilst painful reminiscences and fearful apprehensions flitted across her mind. Kunerick observed a profound silence; and having arrived at the cell, he turned the key and opened the door. But how great was the surprise of Edelbert and Rosa as they entered! Every thing wore an entirely different aspect; they could not recognise the place. It had been changed into a neat, and elegantly arranged place of worship. Two large Gothic windows, with painted glass, fronted the garden in which Rosa and her father had spent many happy hours. The ceiling and walls were painted sky-blue. At one end was a neat little pulpit, and the whole was fitted up with convenient, circular pews.

Edelbert and Rosa expressed their surprise and approbation. "I knew," said Kunerick, "that this alteration would afford you much pleasure. I wished to surprise you, and therefore I did not visit you for some time, nor did I desire you to visit us, until all was finished. Is it not neat, convenient, and beautiful? I, however, lay no claim to any merit in this matter; all the praise and merit is due to my excellent wife. She devised the whole of it, and prevailed upon me to execute her plan. Let me tell you how skillfully she managed this business.

"Last fall, when we returned from a visit to your castle, she asked me to accompany her to the cell in which you were so long imprisoned, and which was consecrated by Rosa's filial affection. I felt but little inclined to go, and said, 'Why do you wish to go there? I feel miserable whenever I think of that cell, and of the cruel and unjust manner in which I treated Edelbert and Rosa!" I could not, however, withstand her appeals, and I accompanied her. When we had entered the place, she said,

"'Only see, my dear husband, how filial affection contrived to transform this once gloomy cell into a pleasant dwelling!"

"'True,' said I, 'it was a dreary and gloomy place, but now it is clean and neat, like a little chapel!'

"'That is a good idea,' replied Hildegard; "it is an idea which first entered my mind, when I saw the little chapel at Linden castle, in which Edelbert, with his family and dependents, worshipped on the Lord's day. This large cell,' continued she, 'might easily be converted into a small place of worship. We might thus show our gratitude to God for the rescue of our child, by doing something for the promotion of his glory, and the God of our fellow-men. Moreover, a chapel is what we really need at our otherwise well-regulated castle; it would exert the happiest influence upon all.'

"The proposition pleased me very much, 'You are right,' said I; 'it shall be so. In this place the sighs and groans of the prisoner shall no more be heard. In this place, we will unitedly thank the Lord for his goodness and mercy manifested towards us, in saving our child from destruction; in bringing about a reconciliation between Edelbert and myself; and in restoring peace to my mind.' These were the circumstances under which this chapel was fitted up."

"And to-morrow," added Hildegard, "our worthy

pastor, Norbert, will dedicate this place to the service of God the Father, Son, and Holy Ghost. Siegbert, Theobald, and other gentlemen of our acquaintance, with their wives and children, have been invited to be present at the dedication. But the guests we chiefly desire on this happy occasion, are you, noble Edelbert, and you, dearest Rosa. I feel assured that you will take a deep interest in the solemnities of the service."

On the next day, the invited guests appeared and took their places in the chapel. Kunerick, his wife and children, with Edelbert and Rosa, on one side of the pulpit, and the invited guests on the other. The other seats were filled with the dependents at Linden and Forest castles, and the peasantry of the neighborhood. After singing of an appropriate hymn, and prayer, the pious Norbert ascended the pulpit, and delivered the following address:

"Beloved hearers:—The love of parents towards a son who was rescued from imminent danger—the love of a pious and devoted daughter towards her father, to whom in this place she so signally displayed her sincere affection—suggested the idea, and was the originating cause of changing this once dreary and gloomy cell into this neat and convenient house of prayer, which we are about to dedicate to the service of God. The circumstances to which we are indebted for the occasion which has brought us together, shall guide me in the remarks I intend to make. A becoming respect for the feelings of my hearers, however, forbids me from entering upon these circumstances in detail. I shall therefore content myself with deducing and illustrating some practical lessons for parents and children.

"It is a beautiful arrangement of Providence, by which the wisdom and goodness of God is strikingly set forth, that has intrusted children—the most helpless and interesting of his creatures upon earth—to the care of kind and affectionate parents; and that he has implanted in the hearts of parents a special love for their offspring—that He communicates to us the first blessings we enjoy in body and mind through the instrumentality of a kind father and an affectionate mother—that He, the invisible God, exhibits to children his infinite love, in a visible and palpable manner, through the love of their parents.

"Oh that all fathers and mothers would use their utmost endeavors to present to their children in their own conduct, a true and correct representation of the goodness and care which God manifests towards them. May they in this imitate God, who not only feeds and clothes, but, in a variety of ways, seeks to instruct them; who, by promises of rewards, would lead them to that which is good, and by threatenings of punishments would deter them from evil; and who, by his various providential dealings with them, would train them for usefulness in life and for happiness and glory hereafter. Oh that the love of parents for their children, that fame of Heaven's kindling, might never be obscured by the smoke and vapor of unhallowed feelings—never degenerate into a blind, carnal affection, which overlooks their faults and errors, and without reproof permits them to go on to ruin. May this love never be perverted by worldliness and vanity, so as to lead parents only to train up their children to shine in the circles of fashion and wealth, and forget their mental, moral, and religious culture.

"Oh that all children might justly appreciate the blessing of having kind, affectionate, and pious parents. Ye sons and daughters who have passed the years of childhood, recall to mind that golden age—those happiest days of your life—and bear in mind what your parents have done for you. They richly provided every thing necessary for your support and comfort. Your food was prepared in due season— your garments made and kept in order by a kind mother. Your fathers endured toils and privations in order to supply your wants, and your mothers were ready to make the greatest sacrifices to render you comfortable. In days of sickness, they watched by your bedside. They warned you of danger. To them you could fly for refuge in times of trouble. They dried your tears. Their wisdom and experience guided your steps. They taught you to speak—they taught you to avoid evil, and to do good. Their approbation and smiles encouraged you to pursue the path of truth and virtue, and even the reproofs which they administered, and the punishments they reluctantly inflicted, were of great advantage to you! How graciously has God cared for you from the first moment of your existence.

"Learn in this wise arrangement of Providence, to acknowledge the goodness of God to you. Honor Him by honoring those parents through whose hands he has shown you so much kindness. Let your bosoms swell with the warmest feelings of gratitude; never be guilty of filial ingratitude, which, while it wounds the parent's heart in its tenderest part, will render you most despicable and vile. Repose a cheerful confidence in your parents, and in every emergency seek their council and advice. Let it be your constant endeavor to render them happy, and, as far as in your power, repay their kindness towards you. As in your helpless infancy and youth, they took care of you, so in the helplessness of their declining years, do you take care of them, and smooth their pathway to the tomb. Rather than suffer your parents to want, you should be content with the meanest fare. Thus will you obey the precept of the Lord: 'Honor thy father and thy mother,' and the promise annexed shall not fail."

A few more practical remarks were made by the worthy pastor, when, after a warm and most earnest appeal to the throne of grace, he bade the congregation rise, and in the most solemn manner said:

"This place, O thou Most High, we now solemnly set apart from all ordinary uses, to the sacred services of the sanctuary. Here let thy name be recorded; here thy presence be manifested; here thy truth proclaimed; and here may many be trained up for usefulness in this world, and for eternal happiness in the world to come, through Jesus Christ. Amen."

After the chapel had been dedicated, the invited guests were conducted into the large hall of the castle, to partake of a collation prepared for them. Scarcely were they seated, when they were aroused by the loud sound of the trumpet. Kunerick and Edelbert ran to the window, and saw a number of well-armed soldiers entering the court-yard. And before he had time to inquire what was the matter, several of his servants entered the hall, and cried, "The duke—the duke." Kunerick and his guests hastened to bid him welcome. The duke was a man of fine appearance, rather tall and slender; his locks were silvered with age, but his eye beamed with all the fire and energy of youth. He first extended his hand to Edelbert, and remarked: "Dearest sir, I have come to announce to you the conclusion of a treaty of peace, on the most honorable terms for our nation. I have also come to tender you the thanks of the emperor, as well as my own, for the effectual aid which the brave soldiers that you were pleased to send us rendered in our conflicts with the enemy. Many of them fell, covered with wounds, upon the field of battle, and I have felt it a duty to accompany, in person, the few who yet remain. At a late hour last evening, we arrived at your castle, where I learned that you were at Forest castle. This morning, at break of day, I hastened to this place.

"My visit," continued he, addressing himself to Kunerick, "is, no doubt, a very unexpected one to you. I have, however, a message from the emperor to you also, expressive of his majesty's gratification with the reconciliation which has taken place between you and the noble Edelbert. I assure you, I can scarcely express the satisfaction I experience in finding you on such friendly terms; and especially to find you assembled on so interesting an occasion.

"I have, besides, a message of great importance for Miss Rosa; but as your dinner has been ready for some time, and my unexpected visit has detained you, I will reserve further communications for the present, and consider myself, Madam Hildegard, as a guest at your amply provided repast.

"You and your friends," replied Hildegard, are most heartily welcome—so please be seated."

Whilst at dinner, the duke remarked: "The news of the taking of Edelbert's castle, of his imprisonment, and of his liberation through the agency of Madam Hildegard, and Miss Rosa, reached us at the imperial camp; but we were not made acquainted with the circumstances in detail. I should be much pleased to hear them, from the actors in this unhappy affair."

"You shall be gratified," replied Kunerick, Hildegard, and Rosa, each in turn. But Edelbert and Rosa, in order to spare the feelings of Kunerick, omitted many circumstances which might place him in an unfavorable light, and reflect upon his character. Kunerick, however, remarked, "You need not conceal any thing; I have erred, and concealment will not mend the matter; it is best to acknowledge our errors, and to endeavor, as far as possible, to make amends for them. I have endeavored to do so, and would recommend a similar course to others, for I am convinced that without it we can never enjoy peace and happiness of mind."

The duke was much gratified to hear the particulars of the transaction, and pleasantly remarked,—"Miss Rosa was the heroine of the whole tragedy, and to her we are principally indebted for the enjoyment of the present occasion. If a reconciliation had not been effected we might at this time be engaged in a severe and bloody contest. For it could not be supposed that the emperor would permit so sincere a friend as Edelbert to remain imprisoned for any length of time. Indeed, it had been already determined that, as soon as the contest with our enemies had been brought to a close, I should march against Kunerick with a strong force, storm his castle, and liberate Edelbert. God be praised that, in his wise and gracious providence, he has, through this estimable young lady, changed Kunerick's feelings and purposes, and thus liberated her dear father without bloodshed."

Rosa, deeply blushing, replied—"My lord! I deserve not the honor thus conferred upon me. All the praise is due to Him who directed all the circumstances connected with this affair. The little bird which flew into the bucket at the well, bore as conspicuous a part in this matter as I did; and contributed as much to the reconciliation of Kunerick and my father, and to prevent the dreadful alternative to which you have alluded."

The pious pastor, Norbert, with deep emotion remarked, "The sentiment which Rosa has advanced is not only correct, but most excellent. A thousand apparently trifling circumstances transpire, in the course of our lives, to which we pay but little attention, but which are productive of the most important results, and determine the lot of hundreds and thousands of our race. The circumstance alluded to by Rosa was not the only one I notice. Who, for example, would imagine that his happiness or misery could depend upon the fact of our having rain, or not, upon a certain day? And yet if it had rained on that day when the sun shone so beautifully, and invited Kunerick's children to play in the yard of the castle, they would, in all probability, have been kept in the castle, and Rosa would not have had an opportunity of rescuing little Eberhard; and, of course, could not have changed Kunerick's mind in regard to her father. And in the storming of this castle many brave men might have lost their lives, and their widows and orphans been plunged in deep distress. Who would consider it possible that the fact of having a particular dish upon the table, on a certain day, would have any influence upon our actions and our condition in life? And yet if that dish of mushrooms had not been on the collier's table, Rosa might never have conceived the idea of entering into service with the wife of the steward; and the happy results accomplished by her would not have been effected. Thus the providence of God is displayed in the apparently unimportant events of our lives. As the skillful musician knows how to unite a variety of sounds, and even introduce occasional discords, in order to produce a most admirable piece of music, so the wisdom of our heavenly Father employs prosperous and adverse circumstances in our lives to accomplish His wise and gracious designs with us. If we would but more frequently and attentively dwell upon the various events which characterize our lives, how often would we find occasion to admire the wisdom and goodness of God displayed in His providence."

The remarks of the pastor were cordially responded to by all, and elicited a highly complimentary reply from the duke.

"And now," continued the duke, "I must deliver the message of the emperor to Rosa. The affection of Rosa for her father, which has led her to undergo so much self-denial, and so many trials; and her noble and heroic act in rescuing Kunerick's son, have gained for her the esteem and friendship of his majesty, the emperor, and determined him to make the following declaration, signed by his own hand, and sealed with

the great seal of the state. Take and read this," said the
duke, handing the document to Rosa. Rosa, however,
was so much overcome by the unexpected honor thus
conferred upon her, that she trembled like a leaf, and
could not read a word. She therefore handed it to one
of the guests, saying, "Read—read." He read as follows:

"Highly respected Miss:—As your father has
no male heir, and the estate of Linden castle is
an entailed property, and must consequently, after
his death, revert to the crown,—therefore, it has
pleased us, as a reward for your father's services,
and for your peculiar excellence of character, to
convey all the right and title of said estate, after
the death of your father, to you, and your family,
for ever. In the event of your marriage, the man of
your choice will not be under necessity of com-
plying with any other condition, in order to enter
upon the possession of the estate, than to assume
the name and title of 'Linden.' And thus may this
honorable name be transmitted from generation
to generation, and this family prove a blessing to
thousands."

(Signed)_____

Edelbert and Rosa were much affected by this dis-
tinguished favor from the emperor, and could scarcely
find words to express their gratitude.

The wish expressed by the emperor was fully realized, for the name of "Linden" was long known, and
ever associated with all that was great and good. Many

young men, of high standing and character, were competitors for the affections of Rosa, but she chose Ekbert, the youngest son of the count, in consequence of his mild disposition, and his piety; and to whom, a short time after the date of our history, she was married. They lived together in harmony and peace, and in the fear of the Lord, beloved by all, and doing good to all.

The duke having expressed a desire to see the well and the chapel, Hildegard bade a servant to place some lights around the rim of the bucket, and have it ready when the duke should come.

After dinner, the company proceeded to the well. Seeing the candles burning, the duke inquired, "What are these for?" Hildegard replied, "In order to show you the great depth of the well." "Truly," said he, as he saw the glimmering lights sinking deeper and deeper, "I am more and more astonished to think that Rosa had courage enough to venture down there. As long as this castle stands, this heroic action will command the admiration of all who hear it. This well will remain as a monument for Rosa, far surpassing all the monuments of statesmen and warriors."

"Nay, my lord, speak not thus," said Rosa, with becoming modesty; "rather say—'This well is a memento of the power and goodness of God.' I am at this moment, while looking into the fearful abyss, fully persuaded that the courage which animated me at the time that I descended into the well, lay not in me, but was imparted by God himself. God saved the boy. Unto Him, from whom every good desire and all good actions do proceed, be all the praise."

From the well they proceeded to the chapel. The duke admired its neatness and convenient arrangement, and remarked, "As Rosa's affection for her father has changed this once gloomy cell into a house of prayer, the inscription, 'IN REMEMBRANCE OF FILIAL AFFECTION,' ought to be set in gold letters upon its walls."

"Never!—never!" replied Rosa; "that would be giving the glory to the creature. To the Lord be all the glory, and to Him alone is this house dedicated. Let the inscription, in letters of gold, and studded with diamonds, be, 'TO OUR GOD, WHO CONTINUALLY DOETH WONDERS.'"

The pious pastor spoke in the highest terms of Rosa's sentiments, and added, "I propose the inscription, in large golden letters,—Honor thy father and thy mother, that thy days may be long in the land which the Lord thy God giveth thee." It was done according to his suggestion; and the promise annexed to this commandment was abundantly realized by Rosa and her family.

**The Children of Cloverley** HESBA STRETTON

Every day, in all the little common things as well as the great ones, we are to do the will of God. But when we love the level of comfort we have attained and the plans we have for the future, it is hard to say, "Thy will be done." The children of Cloverley not only say it—they do it. This dramatic adventure gives hope and courage, and will touch the heart of each family member.

**Little Sir Galahad** LILLIAN HOLMES

*Little Sir Galahad* will capture your heart from the start as you peer into the life of a little boy who can no longer walk. Facing new restrictions and challenges, David learns that real strength comes in controlling his own spirit.

**Tom Gillies** MRS. GEORGE GLADSTONE

Tom Gillies and Dick Potter secretly meet at their favorite cave to concoct their plans for the day and plot the mischievous schemes which have given them so bad a name on Norton Island. The townspeople complain that the island is too small to hold such troublesome boys. Tom is sent away to work, where he learns that his bad habits have fastened strong chains around him, and sin has tied binding knots, making him a prisoner. He discovers the One who can untie those dreadful knots and free him to live a productive life among the people of Norton Island.

**Me and Nobbles** AMY LEFEUVRE

Amy LeFeuvre has done it again! An enchanting story about imaginative Master Bobby and his beloved "friend," Nobbles. With great expectation, Bobby daily awaits his absent father's return, knowing he hasn't been forgotten. In the meantime, Bobby strives to find the secret to obtaining his very own clean white robe so that he can enter the golden gates that lead to the splendid golden city.

**Jessica's First Prayer** HESBA STRETTON

Barefoot little Jessica lives in a home where no one has taught her about God. She looks forward to spending time once a week with Mr. Dan'el, a miserly old coffee peddler who eases his darkened conscience by giving her coffee and stale bread. Jessica's prayers and innocent questions go straight to the coffee peddler's heart. He learns to value the life of a child more than money as he becomes Jessica's new father.

## OTHER LAMPLIGHTER SELECTIONS

**The Stranger At Home**  VARIOUS AUTHORS

*The Stranger at Home*, along with its accompanying stories, might seem a little "hard-edged," but it aptly challenges us to reconsider our God-given roles as parents and children. The folly of permissive parenting, and the inevitable consequences of obstinacy, disobedience, lying, and vanity are brought forth with "not-so-subtle" clarity, yet permeated with life-changing truths.

**Winter's Folly**  MRS. O. F. WALTON

This is the tender story of lonely Old Man Winter, who demonstrates the epitome of selfless love. But all is not lost as young Myrtle, through her childlike innocence, rekindles his desire to live. This true-to-life story reminds us once again that when life seems to hold more than we can bear, we can rest assured that we have a loving God who is orchestrating events for our good.

**Fireside Readings (Vol. I and II)**  VARIOUS AUTHORS

Lamplighter's collection of fireside readings gently instills virtuous qualities such as honesty, integrity, loyalty, courage and perseverance into the very fabric of our lives. Through unforgettable events, common, everyday boys and girls become heroes as they overcome temptation and courageously fight the adversary. Our children will want to be more like them—in fact, they will long to be.

**A Puzzling Pair**  AMY LEFEUVRE

Inseparable twins, Guy and Berry are bursting with creativity and spunk. They are on a mission...to fill Guy's very big picture of the second coming of Jesus with all the people who are ready to meet Him! But his picture must be true, and time is running out! This rather unique approach to evangelism is as pure, bold, and simple as it gets!

**The Mansion**  HENRY VAN DYKE

This little book is a powerhouse, sending a quickening jolt to the very depths of our respectable-looking façade. *The Mansion* takes a piercing look at John Weightman, one of the most "successful" men in New York, and his son, who desperately wants to find his way and be free to make his own mistakes rather than being played like pieces in a game of chess. *The Mansion*...it will make you think.

**Enoch Roden's Training**  HESBA STRETTON

This book is bursting with life's lessons! Through severe trials, Enoch learns much about sound business principles, sacrifice, and trusting God. If he had only said, "I am working with God..." he would never have found his work wearisome, for of all grand, and comforting, and heart-refreshing thoughts in this world, the greatest is the thought that we are co-workers with God. Without a doubt, after reading this book, you'll walk away a better person than when you began.

**Probable Sons**  AMY LEFEUVRE

*Probable Sons* etches into our hearts the importance of forgiveness and reconciliation. The delightful story will keep you smiling as our little heroine Milly boldly and innocently exhorts "probable (prodigal) sons" to return home. May the truths found in this little story find a resting place in the many hearts that have strayed far from home.

**The Wrestler of Philippi**  FANNIE E. NEWBERRY

Here is a story of Rome's staggering contrasts—extreme poverty amidst the wildest extravagance; treacherous dungeon life in darkness; chains amidst the splendors and amusements of luxurious court life. The story's dramatic unfolding will grip your heart as you experience the true test of loyalty and triumph of faith!

**The Inheritance**  CHRISTOPH VON SCHMID

A faithful grandson seeks to find help for his blind grandfather. When the old man finally opens his eyes, he sees a painting on the wall before him and realizes that this is the very house where he buried a wealthy man's inheritance fifty years ago. To their surprise, much more is found than earthly treasure!

LAMPLIGHTER *Publishing*

BUILDING CHARACTER, ONE STORY AT A TIME.

A DIVISION OF CORNERSTONE FAMILY MINISTRIES

To order a catalog, call us toll free at 1-888-246-7735,
email us at mail@lamplighterpublishing.com,
or visit our website at www.lamplighterpublishing.com.